THE LAST
OF THE
SOUL
SEARCHERS

THE LAST
OF THE
SOUL
SEARCHERS

To Lisa and Don, The
Greatest Vintner's in Logan County,
Always taking of my Wino
Family.

David W. Ashby

To order additional copies of this book, contact:
Xlibris
844-714-8691
www.Xlibris.com
Orders@Xlibris.com
828681

PART 1
The Arcturians

The Present Day

CHAPTER 1

I knew he had to die the moment he stepped into my car. The evil in his soul reached out like tentacles from the back seat, wrapping themselves around my beefy neck as they threatened to cut my air supply off. I cleared my throat and cheerfully said, "Welcome to the Burger King Car!" There was a long pause, and finally, the beast spoke, "What in the hell does that mean?"

"Well, you don't get a plant burger, but in my car, YOU GET IT YOUR WAY!" and before I could check on his comfort level, legroom, and temperature, he rudely replied, "Well, okay, silly ass, my way is for you to shut the hell up and drive." As the demon spoke these words, I glanced in the rear-view mirror, and the back seat was partially illuminated by the cell phone it was texting on. This demon's face had a classic mobster's profile, beady pig eyes that popped out of an acne-scarred face. The most noticeable feature of this creature's profile was a scar running from the hairline down its cheek terminating along the jawbone. I studied him for a moment, my exceptional abilities picked up one emotion--anger, a deep sense of hatred for society in general. This demon had a psychopathic urge to make segments of society pay for deep underlying feelings of rage, born of resentment and perceived disrespect. It is what Devin Kelley or Stephen Paddock felt as they slew innocent people at mass shootings in Las Vegas, Nevada, or Charleston, South Carolina.

This being my 5,426th trip over a four-year period as a driver for Goober, an offshoot of the famous Uber company, I professionally responded with a polite, "Yes, Sir," while I reached down on my brand-new Lexus dashboard and touched a small button that would send a microscopic needle into the neck of the beast, releasing enough tranquilizer to make this manifestation of evil sleep for a couple of hours. He would feel nothing, and hopefully, when he woke up, he would be in mid-flight, squirming and kicking his legs in sheer terror.

I drove toward Bentwood, Tennessee, a small bedroom community on the outskirts of Nashville. My client, turned captive, was sound asleep on my leather seats, snoring like a pig with sinus issues. I just hoped the soon-dead man would not drool on my backseat and saturate my seats with his nasty saliva-filled D.N.A. I was heading for the Natchez Hills, a remote area sacred to the Cherokee and Chickasaw Indians.

My hand began to twitch nervously as I thought about having to take another life, but if my intuitions were correct, this hombre was on the verge of a hideous act of violence. I justified it as a vigilante murder, committed by me as an appendage of God himself, taking out demons in human camouflage, sort of like bags of human trash thrown in into the flames of hellfire.

I knew the rally point like the back of my hand, this being my fifth "intervention." I coined the name because my own family had tried on so many occasions to intercede in my own miserable life but failed to convert me. I enjoyed being the black sheep of the family or at least the one that cuts through all the bullshit and tells it like it really was! In my mind I was a frigging hero, helping to keep my narcissist Family Member's massive egos in check. At 11:30 p.m. the desolate country road was deserted, so I pulled off the road by a deserted old barn that was barely standing. I got out and removed the giant plank of timber that acted as a lock on the giant barn doors. I opened the left door and then the right. Both squeaked with a wicked intensity. I looked around half expecting an old leather-faced farmer to materialize with a 12-gauge shotgun pointed at my dome.

Next, I backed my new Lexus carefully into this antique barn from eons ago, and the craziest thought popped into my head, somewhat like the old marriage statement: "Something old, something new, please don't get married or you're screwed."

I quickly cut the engines and turned off the lights. I then climbed in the back seat and put my fingers on sleeping beauty's left solar plexus. The psychic surge of energy almost made me go into convolutions; in fact, I would have bitten my tongue in half, if I had not put my mouthpiece in. I could feel this demon's rage and hatred, directed toward humanity in general but blacks specifically. I felt like I was right beside a demon as he opened the doors to the church, raised his ak47, and sprayed the mostly black congregation with bullets, as Kelley had done in that South Carolina church years before, all the while laughing a wicked, hideous laugh as he shouted racial slurs. I quickly removed my hand from the beast to stop the visions as I shook with unmitigated rage. I knew that I had peered into the future, and this rabid dog had to be put down.

I got out of the car, opened my trunk, and retrieved my signal lights. I lay them in front of the car. These flares from another world began to pulsate, to vibrate, and to glow with an intensity that always amazed me to the core of my soul. A few minutes passed, and the back passenger door flew open. This huge beast of a man began to emerge slivering out of the back seat onto the ground like some weird human snake. He began to moan, his black eyes flew open, and he howled like a werewolf as the tractor beam from the U.F.O. began to lift him off the ground. I watched as his body was lifted higher and higher in the air, his legs and arms moving in a desperate attempt to escape. He resembled a bug caught in a spider's web, moving toward his destiny and karma. I loved this part of my job knowing that the aliens, after retrieving the demon's D.N.A., would reduce his body to a tiny bundle. They would flush it out in space, much like a commercial aircraft would eject frozen blueish human waste out of its lavatories.

I was getting anxious. It had been ten minutes since my customer disappeared into the bowels of the alien craft, and my app was checking to see that I had not been kidnapped or murder. The text read: "According to G.P.S., your car is about twenty miles from destination. Is everything okay?" I knew that I would have to text a reply super-fast or they would send out a B.O.L.O. on my car, and every law enforcement officer within the radius of fifty miles would be searching for me. I texted back, "Yes, customer had forgotten to put a stop on his app, and I should be in route to final destination in ten minutes."

I hate this part of the intervention. It made my heart race and pulse quicken to think about the consequences of my fare just disappearing into the dark heavens. I would not look good in an orange jumpsuit, and I am extremely claustrophobic. Also, I am petrified of big bubba and his midnight visitations with wild love on his mind. Hell, I might even be put in the nuthouse if I told them my story of how the aliens got my rider! I pulled my car out of the barn and waited, nervously playing with my nephew's fidget spinner. Ah, yes, I was indeed feeling fidgety.

The shadow appeared directly to my left and was moving quickly in the direction of my car. All I could think about was Stephen King's pet cemetery when things came back from the dead and then proceeded to go on a murderous rampage. I closed my eyes to pray and then thought the Creator of the Universe must be laughing his head off getting a prayer request from a demon seed such as myself. When my headlights illuminated my rider's extra-large frame, I gasped as I saw an exact carbon copy of the bastard down to the large scar that ran the length of his jawbone that I just fed to the aliens. "Damn!" I thought, "Those frigging aliens have always been one step ahead of the retarded human race. Their cloning process was spot on. He climbed in the back seat, and I could feel his righteousness and sweet soul immediately! All the malevolent evil, all the hideous vibes were gone, replaced by a dude that literally would not hurt a fly.

"Where to?" I asked, making sure his memory and mental facilities were intact.

"Take me to1536 Falcon Crest Way," he answered in a laid-back tone. I decided to test him with my Burger King rant. He replied with a radiant smile that seem to light up the car, "My man, hell, yes! You're going to get five stars and a big tip!"

I smiled to myself, feeling almost heroic. I just saved countless lives and brought an identity into this world that will benefit humanity and protect others instead of taking lives. I drove down the dark, curvy road while talking Tennessee Titan football with my newfound friend, thinking maybe, just maybe, my life was not cursed! I enjoyed my life at that moment, making America great again one life at a time. Imagine me, Shaun MacGregor, royal screw up, being the last of the soul searchers on earth.

CHAPTER 2

Chris Dermott took a little nap during our trip back to his last destination with the help of my microscopic needle filled with a tranquilizer. I checked his neck for visions of his future actions of evil, and I was rewarded with only actions of compassion and empathy for his fellow man. I nudged his shoulder, and he woke up, surprised that he had fallen asleep. He then shook my hand with genuine vigor and handed me a bill with Andy Jackson's picture on it.

He looked me in the eyes and said with great conviction, "Man! You're an awesome driver, and somehow by your kindness, you changed my life."

With a look of sheer gratitude, he hugged me with great intensity, and I will never forget the look in his eyes. It was one of sheer joy because his soul was now set completely free. As I started the engine and waved goodbye, I could not help but wonder if my converts know on some subconscious level the changes in their soul. Now, instead of being bound for hell's fiery death, they were destined for the pearly gates of heaven.

It was nearly three a.m., so I decided to turn my app off. Being my own boss and master of my destiny was one of my favorite benefits of being a driver for hire. I made about $200.00 in three hours, an amount which would nicely supplement my monthly disability check. I looked at the twenty-dollar bill that Chris had handed me, and the lyrics of George Thorogood song "I Drink Alone" echoed through my mind. I knew that tonight I would drink with an exceptionally fine acquaintance of mine -- Johnny Walker and his two cousins, Black and Red. I headed off to the nearest all-night liquor store. Being a good and dedicated alcoholic, I knew its location by heart. As I drove in delirious anticipation of receiving my manna from heaven, I thought it was ironic that I could save souls on this earthly plane but could not save my own pathetic, drunken soul. I began to tremble and tear up as emotions and feelings of a wasted life bubbled up like a flooded stream into my troubled mind.

I traveled back toward Springfield, Tennessee, which was about thirty miles away, all the way fighting the urge not to start the conversation with my bud Johnny Walker, knowing that a D.U.I. would terminate my employment with Goober. I needed that extra income to feed the ravenous hunger of my demons.

I was in my late fifties, living in the basement of my Aunt Jackie and Uncle Jim who were both in their mid-eighties. Uncle Jim had a severe case of glaucoma and could not drive anymore, and Aunt Jackie is in the terrible grip of the beginning stages of dementia. So, I did the heroic and humanitarian thing and moved into their basement so I could be Uncle Jim's driver and give my aunt unconditional love and support. Truth of the matter was I was a total loser, married three times, estranged relationships with my children, and no contact with my young grandchildren. I was on disability for severe heart issues--five bypasses, and a couple of stents, but my spirit, vitality, and strength kept me alive, doing incredible things that defied the medical professionals' opinions that I should have died five years ago.

My life figuratively stopped at the tender age of eleven when the human monsters conspired with Satan to stain my soul and created unending depression and anxiety so horrible that I hid it from others for decades. God made me strong and courageous because He had a mission and a destiny for my life, and until about two years ago, I was totally clueless why He had allowed terrible early events to mold my life.

Chapter 3

Early in October, there was already a heavy frost on the lawn as I pulled my car into my aunt's driveway. The full moon was illuminating the lawn, casting a silver glow on the ground. I heard the crickets in the sugar maple trees that lined the driveway. They seemed to sense my strong desire to initiate my communion with the Walker boys, so there was a quickening of their cadence urging me to begin my journey into oblivion. The light was on in the kitchen of my aunt's house. My beautiful Aunt Jackie was sun-downing, a symptom of the disease that was slowly stealing her mind. The light from the kitchen brightened the path to the back of the house. At least, I had a separate entrance to my mancave. As I stood at the basement door, I listened to the wind whistle through the sugar maples in the backyard and noticed the clouds racing across the sky as if trying to evade capture by some malevolent being. The moon was peeking through the trees, and the sphere was so colossal that I imagined it was the Creator of the Universe holding a flashlight and peering deeply into my soul. As I peered into the bright fall sky, I also knew the Arcturians were peering down on me because they had been watching humanity since the beginning of time.

I silently opened the door to my dwelling and was greeted by my pet Springer spaniel. He jumped so much that I bent down so he could lick my face. His name was Judge after the famous slogan of the sixties, "Here comes the judge!"

"What's up, Judge? Want something to eat, old buddy?" He cocked his head to one side and scurried off to get his dinner bowl, his bobtail furiously wagging. He was my best friend on the entire planet. I looked over my basement crib with pride. All my football trophies sat on a hardwood mantle. I made all-state linebacker my senior year in high school and later played at Western Kentucky University. My coach used to always say, "This is practice, MacGregor. Go half speed. You're killing my starting running backs."

I was a tackling machine then, wanting to inflict as much pain as possible on teammate or foe. Off the field, I was one of the kindest dudes around, always making my friends laugh, but once I set my foot on the practice field or under the stadium lights on Friday nights, it was war. After years of reflection, I knew that it was misplaced, unmitigated rage against the pedophiles who stole my youth that provoked my actions. My heart and goodness were always held captive by the compulsion to prove my manhood repeatedly.

Judge broke my mental pity party by bringing his bowl over to be filled with his favorite cooked liver and pork chops that I kept in my own private kitchen which was complete with a microwave oven and a small refrigerator I had stolen from a cheap motel room in Nashville after drinking too much. I got my buddy Judge his early morning breakfast and turned on the gas stove designed to look like a wood-burning one, hoping that the heat would dispel the chill in the air. I sat on the big leather couch in my apartment and turned on the 64-inch flat-screen television to watch reruns of the *Jimmy Fallon Show*. The fire was making me feel cozy and relaxed, so it was an excellent time to start my long conversation with my ole buddy Johnny Walker.

Suddenly, the door flew open at the top of the stairs, and I lurched off the couch, as I heard a gurgled, raspy voice from the bowels of hell say, "Shaun, I'm coming to rape you, dissect you, and eat you like a tasty morsel."

I hastily got under the couch, and my rational mind whispered to my subconscious, "You are a grown man. You are too big to crawl underneath a couch."

I then looked at my image in the mirror above the television, and much to my horror, I was an eight-year-old boy again. My heart was pounding in my chest. I could hear footsteps coming down the stairs.

As the putrid smell of rotting flesh filled the air, I instinctively knew this beast was a hitman from hell, finally coming to make me pay for my sins.

I heard it continuing down the stairs, its breathing sounded like a roaring storm heading in my direction as I peered out from underneath the sofa and as fear was coursing through every cell in my body.

Suddenly, it was standing in the middle of my den. Large tentacles were where feet should have been. Big reddish scales covered its entire body, and puss mixed with saliva was running down and pooling on the hardwood floor directly in front of me. The most horrifying image was the two heads of the beast which looked human and awfully familiar. They were positioned in such a way that the beast could scan 360 degrees. My pulse began to quicken. The panic was causing me to hyperventilate.

Just as I was about to scream, I felt a tentacle wrap around my leg. I tried to yell, but no sound escaped my throat. The tentacle tightened and began to pull me away from my protective cover under the couch. I was dragged out into the open, completely vulnerable and at the mercy of his hellhound. The two heads looked down at me with a look of lust and hunger as it snarled showing large carnivorous fangs. It reached for me with an appendage that looked like hooks of rotting flesh.

They were an inch away from my face when I woke up. Sweating and disoriented, I opened my eyes. A sigh of relief escaped from me, and my body relaxed. My eyes scanned the room. I noticed the empty bottle and then realized that like all my other friends, Johnny had deserted me in my hour of need.

Judge was staring at me intently with what seemed to be a look of deep compassion and empathy. As I petted him and assured him his buddy was going to be alright, the random thought came into my mind that his look of caring was more intense than any look my three wives had ever displayed for me.

CHAPTER 4

The terminology of my apartment as a "basement dwelling" is slightly inaccurate. The front portion of my quarters are underground, but because of the downhill slope of the terrain, the back half is above ground. It is half basement and half downstairs, so natural sunlight could filter into my dark subterranean cave in the daylight hours. I thought the sunlight streaming under my shut bedroom door was nature's way of waking up my pathetic drunk ass. I stirred and turned over to notice the golden glow underneath my closed door. I knew that I had overslept again. I glared at my alarm clock, and noticed, in my drunken stupor, that I had not set it. I reached for my cell phone on the cedar bedstand next to my comfortable queen-sized bed, complete with pillow-top mattress. The bed had conspired with Johnny Walker to render me unconscious for twelve hours. It was almost three p.m.! I shook the cobwebs from my brain and looked down at Judge lying on the bearskin rug beside my bed.

"How come you let me oversleep, Judge? You supposed to lick my face when I overdrink."

Judge grunted and looked up at me with his head cocked to one side as if to say, "You are a grown-ass man. I'm not here to babysit you!"

I quickly walked across the tiled floor, which resembled a chessboard, to the bathroom and the shower that would help revive me to a less zombie-like state. As the hot water streamed down my face, my mind began to clear, and I remembered parts of the nightmare that I suffered through the night before. But I only remembered parts of that nightmare; the two human faces made a lasting horrifying impression though.

The hot water stimulated the neurons in my brain, clearing the cobwebs from the night before. Finally, my semi-drunken mind made connections, and despite the hot water running down my back, goosebumps appeared on my arms as my conscious and subconscious mind both agreed that the human faces on that beast in my nightmare matched the faces of the two pedophiles who had molested me as a child.

I went into my room and changed into my work clothes, which included my Titan jersey and sweatpants. One of the great benefits of being a driver for hire is the freedom to dress like some homeless person. Anyway, no client could see the lower portion of my body at night. Besides, many of them were so drunk they could not see my bare ass if I waved in front of them. It was Sunday afternoon, and the Tennessee Titans were at home, playing a late afternoon game, so tonight was going to be extremely busy and very profitable. I strapped on my Nikes and bounded up the stairs with the energy and zeal of a younger man.

Uncle Jim was lying in his recliner, consumed in his favorite pastime-napping. His finger was on his nose as if he were concentrating on a complex math problem.

Uncle Jim was a big man. His chest was massive from pumping weights all his life. He proudly told me that he could bench press over 400 pounds in his prime. He was sporting about a week's growth of gray stubble on his chin, and his hair was cut in the classic crew cut that had been fashionable in the sixties. He wore a muscle t-shirt, which some rural rednecks proudly refer to as a "wife-beater." The words tattooed on his left shoulder were "Semper Fi," meaning "always faithful," indicating Uncle Jim had been in the United States Marine Corps for thirty years. The words "Carpe Diem" or "seize the day" were tattooed on his right shoulder, the saying expressing how my uncle lived his life, always achieving, traveling, and living fully. He barely survived the winter of 1950 when his unit the 5th Marine division was pinned down at Chosin Reservoir during the Korean War. The "Chosen Few" defeated the Chinese at Yudam-ni, but at the cost of over 11,000 lives, many of the casualties dying from exposure from extreme cold or starvation. Uncle

Jim won the Congressional Medal of Honor and a Purple Heart for his heroic actions during the seven-day siege.

I tried not to wake my uncle because I knew he would chastise me for sleeping well into late afternoon. Uncle Jim had been a drill instructor after the war and did not like any sign of weakness or laziness. Unfortunately, his senses were still so sharp that my attempt to worm my way into the kitchen failed miserably.

"About time you got up, tenderfoot. I was getting ready to call the undertaker to collect your corpse," Uncle Jim's voiced thundered across the room like a sudden spring storm. His bright blue eyes sparkled with humor and vitality. He reached out to tap my leg as I walked by. Uncle Jim was like my older brother, and I would take a bullet for him. I know he would return the favor in a heartbeat.

Aunt Jackie was in the kitchen, cooking up my favorite breakfast--homemade blueberry pancakes and turkey bacon. I grabbed a plate and gave her a big kiss on her cheek, asking her how my favorite aunt was doing this morning. She laughed knowing that she was my only aunt. She was still a beauty at 83 with striking emerald green eyes much like her husband's, still full of youth and vitality even after 60 years of marriage. She had the high cheekbones and skin that a 25-year-old model would have been jealous of.

"How would you like your coffee, honey?"

Before I could answer, my Uncle Jim, not wanting to miss an opportunity to deliver a punchline, shouted from the living room, "Baby, you know he likes his coffee like his women--black and hot."

I laughed heartily like it was the very first time that I heard that lame joke. You know that people love you when they continue to laugh at the same stupid shit you say.

I answered my aunt with a gentle voice, "Aunt Jackie, despite what your obnoxious hubby says, I will take a little cream and sugar." I knew that Uncle Jim was going to add. "Like a little wuss," and two seconds later I heard Uncle Jim mutter to himself, "Like a little wuss." I chuckled to myself. It seemed like I was stuck in my favorite Bill Murray's movie *Groundhog Day*, reliving the same day so many times that I could predict events and conversations before they occurred.

"So, honey, are you going to Dallas today. . . to pick up your clients? You know they will all be so drunk after the Cowboys win," she exclaimed, her eyes glowing with exhilaration or madness.

Uncle Jim and my aunt had lived in Dallas for twenty years, and my heart ached for my aunt because she wanted to remain in the years in which she was in full command of her formidable mental focus and abilities.

I gently responded to her, "Yes, Aunt Jackie. Going to be working in Nashville, picking up Titans' fans."

She suddenly changed into a person that I had never known. "I hate those fucking Titans. They suck!" she exclaimed with a nasty snarl.

I smiled and calmly said, "Now, Aunt Jackie, tell me how you really feel."

Deep down I knew she responded with such venom because she was embarrassed by her own confusion. My Aunt Jackie was an immensely proud woman.

"You be careful because I love you like a son," she said as she scurried off to do more household chores, like changing the bed linens, mopping and sweeping the floors, and cleaning out the garage, even though she had completed the exact same tasks the day before.

I was devouring my precious pancakes when I heard a knock at the door. I knew that Uncle Jim and Aunt Jackie would not hear the obnoxious pounding, and judging by the powerful knocking, I knew that it was my best friend from high school, Johnny "Pee Wee" Miller. Pee Wee was pre-safety on our state champion football team our senior year and an All-Southern Kentucky Conference shortstop on our baseball team. He was short compared to my 6'3" frame but was powerfully built with massive biceps and wide square shoulders. His pale blue eyes and blond hair seemed to hint at Nordic heritage. He had massive legs with bulging calves and quads, even at our age. At 5'8" he could dunk a basketball easily because of a vertical leap of a couple of feet. His leaping ability led to many interceptions on the gridiron. Like most athletes that are hometown heroes, Johnny peaked at eighteen and lived his life perpetually caught in his "Glory Days."

Johnny originally had thought they called him Pee Wee after the great Pee Wee Reese who had played shortstop for the Brooklyn and later Los Angeles Dodgers from 1940-1958. Unfortunately, Johnny's many girlfriends gave him the obnoxious nickname, after viewing his manhood. Johnny was my best friend, so I always tried my best to shield him from the truth, but some cold-hearted bitch at the senior homecoming party spilled the beans. My friend Johnny was shattered, and for thirty-five years, he has tried every drug, like Extensa, and every other therapy known to man.

I opened the door and was met with the biggest, mindless grin. "How you doing, old buddy? I got the Madden 2019 NFL football game, and a brand-new *Call of Duty* Xbox game," Pee Wee said with great gusto and excitement.

I just stared at him in disbelief, my adult friend still wanted to play Xbox down in my basement, like he was about ten years old. I looked at the man-child whose emotional growth had been stunted and felt empathy for him.

I knew that I had to be in Nashville in two hours, but I couldn't bear to hurt Pee Wee's feelings, so I calmly said, "Get your sorry ass downstairs. I guess I have time to punish your arse for one game. Damn, you are a glutton for punishment. Don't you ever get tired of getting your ass whipped?"

He gleamed at me with appreciation and gloated, "Not today, my man. Gonna be the Green Bay Packers, and Jerry Rodgers is gonna light your pass defense up!" We both laughed in unison because neither one of us believed his bullshit.

Uncle Jim was sound asleep again; however, being almost ninety and having dutifully served our country, that entitled him to spend his time anyway he wanted to. We bounded down the stairs, like a couple of overgrown kids, trading barbs that ranged from chastising each other's skills to downright ribbing each other on our shortcomings in intelligence. Judge just loved Pee Wee and was overly excited to see his old friend. He jumped on Pee Wee like a middle linebacker, almost knocking him down. Judge's bobtail was wagging with great vigor as he licked Pee Wee's face. I guess dogs can sense a pure heart because my friend Pee Wee had the biggest heart of any person that I have ever known.

I chose the Tennessee Titans as my team and set the time for twelve-minute quarters. Pee Wee complained about the abbreviated time, but I ignored him, explaining that some folks had to work. We were only about ten minutes into the game when Pee Wee started talking about his favorite subject--aliens and abductions.

"Hey, man, did you know that Area 51 in Roswell, New Mexico, actually has preserved alien lifeforms on the base?" he mumbled as he moved his joystick in an aggressive manner, trying to put a jarring hit on my starring running back Jermaine Henri. I just nodded my head in a conforming gesture of surrender, as I prepared for the next thirty-minute onslaught of alien history and human cover-ups of alien encounters. My friend Pee Wee was a serious conspiracy theorist. He even believed that the government was tracking our every movement with G.P.S. devices implanted under our skin.

"Recently there have been numerous newspaper accounts of U.F.O. sightings all over the globe. Many YouTube videos, too. How do you explain that, professor?" he asked arching his eyebrows in a dramatic fashion.

"Well, Pee Wee, it's a bunch of people seeking attention or being bored with their lives or who are just plain nuts," I replied as I sacked his quarterback for the millionth time.

"Okay, smartass, what about trained military pilots, men responsible for multi-million-dollar fighter jets, reporting objects that can travel twice the speed of sound?" Pee Wee asked as his quarterback fumbled on the five-yard line.

"Have you ever heard of Project Bluebook?" he continued, moaning as I scored another touchdown, making the score 24-zip. I shook my head no, even though he had told me the same thing many times. I figured it was good therapy for him to explain his preoccupations and keep him distracted from the ass whopping he was currently receiving.

"Well, it's a research project initiated by the Air Force in 1952 that discredits many of the pilots that reported strange occurrences in the heavens. Project Bluebook also dispersed secret agents to enforce the silence. They were called the "men in black," accurately depicted by Tommy Lee Jones and Will Smith in the 1980's movie.

"Many folks that claimed they had been abducted say they have been visited by these government agents and have had their memories erased. These aliens, preparing for an invasion, performed many exploratory surgeries, trying to pinpoint weakness or physical vulnerability in the human species," Pee Wee said, increasing the pitch of his voice for dramatic effect. I always thought he should have been a member of the drama club in school.

"Hey, Pee Wee, I think *you* have been abducted by aliens," I said arching my eyebrows towards the heavens.

"You do?" he asked.

"Yeah, man, the aliens performed a frontal lobotomy on you. That's why you're brain dead and getting beat 35 to 7. We both laughed at my quick wit.

Judge's head was lying on Pee Wee's lap. He perked up and turned his head sideways as if to say, "You two are a couple of morons."

"Dude, we are not alone in the vastness of this universe. Do you really believe that we are the only life in a galaxy that goes on forever?" he asked.

"I don't know, but you're going to be alone in the sorrow of your vicious defeat because I have to hit the mean streets of Nashville and make some coin," I said standing up and putting on my shoes back on.

"Okay, man, I can take a hint. Love you, bro. Be safe out there," he said as he grudgingly stood up.

We climbed the stairs to the top floor, and I gave my brother a soul shake, as he was heading out the door. He had absolutely no idea that I was the last soul searcher on earth and that I have had many encounters with a race not of this world. I felt bad about concealing the truth from him, but I was doing it for his protection. I did not realize it then, but there was not a power on earth that would protect my friend from his hideous fate.

CHAPTER 5

I grabbed the keys to my baby and said good-bye to Aunt Jackie, who wanted to know if I was on my way to my apartment. I calmly and patiently explained to her for the tenth time that I was going to Nashville to work and would be home early in the morning.

I kissed her forehead and tapped my Uncle Jim's shoulder, trying not to wake him from his beauty sleep. I stepped into my sleek, black Lexus LS 600 HL, my mobile office for the next eight hours. I open my Goober app on my seventh-generation cell phone and set my destination for Nissan Stadium, home of the Tennessee Titans. I was rewarded with a rider request from White House, Tennessee, a small hamlet about thirty miles northeast of Nashville.

The G.P.S. quickly calculated the route, and I set my phone inside the holder on the dashboard. The trip had no "surge" or an extra incentive associated with it but would pay me almost sixty-five dollars. Since I was going in that direction anyway, it made great business sense not to drive a passenger-less car 65 miles or to borrow the trucker slogan, to "make no bread when I have to deadhead."

I arrived at my pickup location and was greeted by an extremely large client with his equally massive girlfriend. I knew it was going to be an interesting trip because Brian had a Titans' jersey on, while his girlfriend was sporting a Pittsburgh Steelers' jersey. Jennifer, whose name I would later learn, looked like she could play middle linebacker for her Steelers, the Titans' victim of the week. I prayed for the suspension and struts in my new car, as their humongous gluteus maximi contacted my seats.

I have never been known for my sensitivity. I delivered my rant about having everything their way--music, temperature, and available phone charging ports. Brian asked me for an aux cord and some privacy as he glared at his lady. They seemed to be in a heated, passionate discussion about the game, trying to outargue each other about strategies that would allow their favorite team to be victorious. I use the Burger King rant to gauge the degree of social interaction the client expected, and I could sense these two just wanted some privacy. I raised the privacy curtain between the front and back seats to allow these water buffalos to do God-only-knows-what in my back seat.

As I drove on I-65 South toward Nashville, I reflected on the night's potential earnings and my great fortune of living near a major metropolitan area deep in the heart of Dixie. Nashville was the heart and soul of country music and offered not only the Grand Ole Opry, but also the Country Music Hall of Fame and Museum, and by God, if you even consider yourself a Country Music fan, you have to visit Nashville at least once in your lifetime. That pilgrimage to Nashville for a country music fan seemed to be as great as a Muslim's desire to make one to Mecca or Medina once in their lifetimes. Nashville, however, was much more than just the Country Music capital. This dynamic city offered historical landmarks such as the Hermitage--Andrew Jackson's home--and the Belle Meade Plantation.

I was lost in thought, my mind reflecting on the fact that Nashville was a very progressive and dynamic city, offering not only the fine arts, which are showcased at the Frist Fine Arts Center but also classic music at the Schermerhorn Symphony Center. As I crossed over the John Seigenthaler Pedestrian Bridge which spans the very deep Cumberland River, I was transfixed by the beauty of Nashville's skyline as the setting sun sent a crimson rainbow down from the heavens to touch the sparkling waters of the river. My almost Zen-like state was interrupted by two things--the honking of the car behind me urging me to drive faster into the obvious traffic jam 100 yards in front of me and Jennifer's huge moon-shaped face peering over the privacy curtain. Her face had a deep, post-sex flush, and I then sadly realized that the rocking of my car as we zipped down I-65 was not caused by the wind.

"Hey, Goober man, what is the name of the river that we just passed over?"

I wanted to ignore her idiotic question, but my professionalism and concern over my ratings compelled me to answer an obvious setup.

"That's the Cumberland River, which is over forty-feet deep in the section we just crossed over," I replied, giving her clearer information, and hopefully stifling any more absurd inquiries.

"You're so knowledgeable, Mr. Goober man. Can you name the rivers that merge around my hometown?" Jennifer asked like I was a student in some lame geography class.

To her utter surprise, I answered, "Of course, my dear. That would be the Monongahela, Allegheny, and Ohio Rivers. The Monongahela and Allegheny merged to form the Ohio River, which travels 981 miles and terminates in Cairo, Illinois." Geography had been my major at Western Kentucky University, just north of our present location across the state line.

"Wow, you're pretty intelligent for a Goober driver. We have three rivers to your one. It's a sign from God we are going to win by a two-touchdown margin today," she ribbed. She quickly closed the privacy curtain. I chuckled to myself about her simplistic reasoning but shuddered at the fact that she had made a brilliant earth-shattering prophecy, in her mind at least.

I glanced down to my right and noticed the showboat *The General Jackson* dropping off many Titans' fans, who had just enjoyed a gourmet meal and drinks, while touring the Cumberland. It was a pre-game ritual for many late Sunday afternoon games for those who were wealthy C.E.O.s from companies like Nissan, Vanguard Health Systems, and H.C.A., holdings with corporate headquarters in Nashville. The sun gleamed off the AT&T Building, nicknamed the Batman Building because of the two ear-like pointed towers at the very top. I lowered the sun-visor and put on my shades. I stopped my car about half a block from the stadium, hoping that my clients would not have heart attacks lumbering toward the stadium. I unlocked the back doors and thanked them for choosing Goober.

"Thanks, man, great ride. I will tip you on the app," Brian bellowed as he and his lady walked down the street hand and hand, completely oblivious to the looks of disgust from other fans. I watched them for a brief second until they were swallowed up by the sea of humanity heading for the front gate. I wondered why some folks had no understanding of how physically or mentally screwed up they were. It was like some virus had infected mankind thousands of years ago and insulated us from our own pride, arrogance, and stupidity.

The Goober app was lit up again, showing surges ranging from two and a half to six in the outlining suburbs of Nashville, meaning that I would receive from two-and-a-half- to six-times the base fare. It was going to be a very lucrative night. The first ping was a pickup near Centennial Park, which was the only park in the South that had an exact replica of the Greek Parthenon, complete with a statue of Athena, Goddess of Wisdom, Strategy, and Warfare. The Parthenon doubled as an art museum. It was about half a mile from Vanderbilt University, a school for the intellectually gifted and decidedly wealthy from across the country. The pickup location was only about two and a half miles from my location, but because of traffic, my app indicated that it would take me about twenty minutes to get there. The base fare was five bucks, but the surge was around 5.0, meaning I would make around thirty bucks for a two-mile trip. I would have to deal with obnoxious drunks, hookers, and pissed-off Pittsburgh Steelers' fans, upset and outraged by being beaten by a last-minute touchdown pass thrown by Darren Miller, the Titans' third-string quarterback, but I would have made almost 600 bucks in eight hours. I figured that I could not have made that kind of money selling crack, so I reached to set my Goober app to pick up rides that were heading toward Springfield, Tennessee, and my cozy basement apartment. Before I could change the location, the app pinged for a pickup at a seedy bar off Music Row. It was almost one o'clock in the morning, and I was going to ignore it and go home, but a supernatural voice from the Arcturians, or from God himself, commanded me to accept the ride.

CHAPTER 6

The name of the bar was called The Wrong Turn on East Washington Street, a dive frequented by the criminal element that Nashville tried to hide. The customer's destination was almost thirty minutes to my south, so given the surge of 3.5, I would make a cool hundred dollars. I cursed myself for being so greedy and headed toward a ride that I would never forget. Although I was exhausted and badly needed a drink, I obeyed the internal commands that seemed to dominate my soul and headed toward my destiny. I stopped the car in front of the well-lit bar and locked my car doors because of the homeless vagrants, drug addicts, and ladies of the night soon gathering around my car like I was giving away food stamps.

I saw him coming out of the bar--big, burly, and mean-looking. He stopped outside the bar, grabbed a pretty, young lady, and slapped her hard across the face. I almost pressed the accelerator to the floor and squealed out of there as if I had just robbed the place. I just could not move, almost like I was trapped in a nightmare and was frozen with fear, but it was not fear but dedication to a mandate sent down from the universe to rid humanity of this specific despicable creature. I knew right away that he was a pimp although he did not fit the stereotype of having dreadlocks, gold teeth, and a fur coat. Ben Dixon was a large-framed man who looked like he had just ridden a horse across the western plains of Texas. He had a black Stetson cowboy hat on his huge cranium, a stonewashed Western shirt that was tucked into faded blue jeans. A black belt encircled his slender waist, the belt fitting into a large brass buckle that had the likeness of a large bison as its centerpiece. He had on snake-skinned cowboy boots that must have cost several thousand dollars. Ben Dixon was a pimp designed to fit into the Southern culture, a venomous snake camouflaged to inflict evil on unsuspecting victims. As soon as he stepped into my car, he felt the need to explain why he slapped the young prostitute.

"Damn, new Philly! I just picked her up at the bus station. She charged a john only half of what he should have paid. Hey, Goober man, bet you made a fortune tonight with the Titans beating the favored Steelers. How about me setting you up with one of my fine, young Phillies?"

I just ignored his question and did not even ask him about his comfort level. If I had to be nice to this vile creature, I think I would have puked.

"Brother, I am worth a fortune. Got a great business here in Music City. I pick up young runaways at the bus station, and they all have stars in their eyes, wanting to be the new Reba, Dolly, or Taylor. I tell them that I am an agent. Even have my own business cards with a phone number that my other whores answer, acting like my secretaries." Then, the demon laughed--a hideous, wicked laugh straight from the depths of hell.

I get them high and break them in with a group of my closest friends. You know, a gangbang. Film it and post it all on the dark web. That way I am not only breaking them in but getting residual income every time someone logs on and watches. Man, got to have that stream of cash on a constant basis," the bastard boasted.

"Hey, Goober man, I can send you a link to a couple of sessions starring yours truly. They didn't call me Long Dong Silver in high school for nothing," he said, his large face beaming with macho pride.

I just could not stand his mouth any longer. If I had to listen to anymore, I would have to pull over and beat this moron to death. I needed to practice self-discipline; however, I did not want to get on the bad side of my alien brothers. So, I pressed the button that would send a microneedle full of trazodone into his bounteous neck. He was in mid-sentence, bragging about being a multi-millionaire when the trazodone kicked in and knocked him out colder than my vicious left hook would have.

I drove to my intervention point and placed my fingers on his solar plexus. I was transported into a smelly room, watching three men viciously rape and sodomize a young girl of no more than fourteen years old. I could suddenly feel her pain, anguish, and fear. My heart was breaking for her as I watched in horror as they not only ripped her body apart but her soul as well. I heard her screams and could feel the bile build in my throat as my mind regressed in time to my own rape. I felt so much rage that my heart was racing, and my own adrenaline was pumping so fiercely that I do not remember striking the pimp with all my might. I broke his nose, spilt his lip, and was determined to kill him with my bare hands. Repressed rage blinded me and was going to turn me into a killer. As I raised my hand to send this earth-bound demon back to the hellfire from which it had come, my hands froze in mid-air like some invisible force held my arm. I voice came out of nowhere and said, "Vengeance is mine...." I'm not sure if it was the Arcturians or God himself, but suddenly all the fury and rage were gone, and I lowered my hand.

I was gasping for breath and sweating profusely as I got out of the backseat and resumed my mission. I placed the pulsating flairs in front of the car and waited. I looked in the backseat and was shocked at the damage I had done to Dixon's face. I watched for the rise and fall of his chest, half hoping that he was dead, thus saving me precious time. When I saw his body begin to twitch and move, I knew that the alien tractor beam had his beaten, half-dead body in its grip. He looked like a zombie in a C-class Hollywood flick as the tractor beam lifted him higher and higher into the moonlit night. I sat and waited and then began to be frightened as time went on. Perhaps I had killed him, and the aliens could not extract viable D.N.A. Suddenly there was a bright red flare that raced across the sky, and I knew that Ben Dixon would not be cloned. He was just too evil, not enough goodness in his soul to be recycled or cleansed. I would have to take evasive action quickly, or I would be in an orange jumpsuit locked away for the rest of my life.

There would be no time for drinking tonight. I headed for Dixon's drop-off location, 134 Woodlawn Avenue, an upscale neighborhood in south Nashville. I arrived at approximately three a.m., looking for any cameras that could record me and thus act as a witness to my dropping off a ghost. When I was completely satisfied no camera was recording me, I opened the back door and stood on the street for a few minutes, ushering the apparition from my car. The wind was kicking up, and the trees were dropping their leaves. That seemed to be nature's attempt to shield me from the prying eyes of neighbors. I took this as a sign from God--or the aliens or whomever-- that he was pleased with me and wanted to protect me.

I had to get home and reverse my car's video to show a healthy Brian Dixon stepping out of my car at 134 Woodlawn Avenue and disappearing into the night. I was a master at video manipulation and would create a deep fake that the C.I.A. itself would be proud of. I also instinctively knew that no one would file a missing person's report on Brian Dixon because he was just a piece of worthless excrement stuck on the shoe of humanity.

CHAPTER 7

It was sleeting when I arrived at my Aunt Jackie's. The tree branches were bending as the weight of the ice accumulated on them. The moonlight was peeking through the clouds, causing the ice to glow brilliantly on the tree limbs. I paused for a moment, thinking I was the centerpiece in a children's Christmas snow globe, and soon the kids would shake the globe and a burst of snow would bury me alive. Wow, I had not drunk a drop, yet I wondered why that random thought penetrated my consciousness. Maybe it was just the stress and horror of dealing with a complete sociopath like Brian Dixon.

I opened the trunk, got out a plastic tarp, and gingerly placed it over the front window to prevent ice build-up. I then pulled the windshield wipers out and trudged to my apartment. I opened the door, and Judge almost knocked me down, wild with excitement--or sheer hunger.

"How are you doing, old boy? I missed you!" I said as I rubbed the back of his head, then kneeled and gave him a hug. Suddenly, I had a vision of hugging one of my young grandchildren with the same intensity, and tears welled up in my eyes. I am getting unbelievably soft because of my recent "jobs." My younger self would have slapped the shit out of me, and said, "Damn, quit acting like an old woman and go buy some good stout bourbon."

I filled Judge's bowl with food and went into my production studio. After an hour and a half of cutting and pasting the video from my car cam, I had successfully produced something showing Brian Dixon exiting my car at three a.m. on 134 Woodlawn Avenue. Nothing out of the ordinary. It was almost five a.m., and I could hear the sleet pellets hit the windowpane. I knew that I could sleep well into the afternoon since I did not do a damn thing on Mondays, especially in weather like this. I had been on disability for three years, and I still hated Mondays despite the fact now I did not have to get up and go to a regular job! After years of working, Monday's curse hangs on like a mistress that will not go away.

I crawled into my bed and congratulated myself for not drinking a drop, but then the curse of insomnia crept in beside me. I began to think of Mad Dog MacGregor, my stepfather, who had been a career United States Air Force officer and one of the strangest, most secretive, and anal-retentive persons that I had ever known. I never knew my biological father until a couple of years ago. I was cursed from the very beginning of my life--some bastard child with the genetic makeup of a pathetic loser at best or at worst potentially some demonic, cannibalistic killer like Jeffery Dahmer. My mother was a saint, though maybe somewhat fallen, a career educator with a heart of gold, dogmatically dedicated to following Jesus's teachings.

My mother was Catholic and a hundred percent Irish. Her parents, Chris O'Toole and Cheryl O'Brien, meet by chance on the streets of Dublin. They produced a fiery redheaded Celtic goddess named Katherine, my mother. Her brilliant emerald eyes burned with a passion and zest for life that was almost supernatural. Then-Lieutenant Mad Dog MacGregor, ex-fighter pilot, did not stand a chance against the charismatic, social dynamo after my mother set her sights on him at an Alpha Delta Pi sorority mixer at the University of Kentucky. Mike, the "mad dog" fighter pilot, who earned his nickname early in the Vietnam Conflict was smitten with my mother the very first time they met, quickly falling madly in love. My mother explained that she was a package deal and had a four-year-old son, but it did not matter to the lovestruck Mad Dog. The young R.O.T.C. instructor and mature, older college student of twenty-five were married one year later.

My mind was working in overdrive, as I thought about how I inherited my stepfather's name, but not his heart. In his mind, I was the proverbial redheaded stepson. Oh, he hid his rejection of me from my mother, who lived in a dream world, enamored by the lavish lifestyle that a young, handsome Air Force officer could provide for her. On occasion, she would question his hard discipline tactics, and he would always answer, "My discipline and standards produce an adult who is tough and resilient. Shaun will thank me when he gets older because when others fail, he will succeed." I was a tough Irish lad and never complained about the harsh, controlling techniques that deeply influenced my emotional health and self-esteem.

We lived in several states--Nebraska, South Carolina, Texas. I was always jealous of small-town kids who lived in the same town all their lives. Their friendships seemed to be deeper and more intimate. Mine were superficial, my knowing that in a year or two, I would never see their faces again. The combination of sheer loneliness and low self-esteem would lead to my love affair with alcohol. In our residence in Izmir, Turkey, the attraction to booze led to an incident near the ancient aqueducts. That incident changed me forever.

The more I tried to sleep, the more sleep evaded my grasp. I looked down at my best friend, and he was sleeping like a newborn pup.

"Oh, the sleep of the innocent and pure of heart!" I thought. I tossed and turned and thought about that day when I learned that we were moving to Turkey, half a world away. I remember the cultural shock of flying halfway around the world and seeing the beautiful port city of Izmir, a crucial port city on the Aegean Sea even in ancient times. From my window seat on the plane as we circled the once Greek city of Smyrna, I noticed ancient Greek ruins in the hills surrounding the city. The first night we were there, I could hear the elegant mosques with their calls to prayer and see men with sweepers cleaning horse crap off the streets, as the old carriages transported tourists and passengers throughout the city. I suddenly realized, like Dorothy, I was not in Kansas anymore.

I was twelve years old then, and my stepdad had been assigned to the Cryptologic Center in Izmir. It was an assignment critical to the security of the United States since the Cold War with the Soviet Union was becoming very intense. Mike MacGregor, now a full, bird colonial, would supervise forty techs as they spied on the Russians from fortified rooms inside of a mountain. These techs, all with top-security clearances, would use codes obtained by covert operations to track Russian troop movements and placement of I.C.B.M.s. Colonial MacGregor was an extremely strict boss. Any minor infraction of his rules brought swift action through the Uniform Code of Military Justice, ranging from demotion in rank to court-martial. The fact that Mad Dog was my stepfather did not help my popularity status, and the only kid that would hang out with me was Duncan "Speedy" Davis who was my teammate on our youth football team. Speedy played tailback, and I was the starting quarterback, so we bonded like brothers.

One fateful day that changed me forever, Speedy and I were drinking beer near the ancient Roman aqueducts, which my stepfather had repeatedly warned me were strictly off-limits. I was very rebellious and enjoying my freedom as well as a feeling of power from disobeying the colonial's wishes. Speedy asked me, "What do you think Mad Dog would do to you if he caught your ass here?"

I answered with my best John Wayne impersonation, "Well, I tell you what, Pilgrim, frankly I don't give a damn," I said, switching from John Wayne to Rhett Butler while taking a large pull on my Tuborg beer.

Speedy laughed and punched my arm, "That's what I like about you, Shaun. You're a true rebel."

Before I could respond, they were upon us. One slipped his massive, hairy arm around my neck. The other got Speedy in a headlock, choking him till the saliva ran down his chin. Suddenly Speedy slammed his foot down on the attacker's foot.

The pedophile beast screamed a curse in Turkish and momentarily let my friend go. That is the only thing Speedy needed to escape. Living up to his name, he lunged toward the fence. Within seconds, he was over, screaming at the top of his lungs for the Military Police. As I reflect on that day, I know that Speedy saved my life because the cavalry would have never shown up to rescue me if Speedy had not escaped. Before my rescuers appeared, I was half dragged, half carried to a small building underneath the aqueducts and for half an hour was repeatedly sexually assaulted by these demons. To me, they resembled ancient

Ottoman soldiers with bulging forearms, large chests, and foreheads that protruded like Neanderthals.

The biggest began slapping me hard, trying to break my will and force me into complete submission when a round from an m24 sniper rifle pierced his occipital lobe. The second round fired almost simultaneously blew off a portion of the other monster's frontal lobe. Finally, the Air Force police arrived with my friend Speedy in tow. I will never forget the look of horror on their faces as the Air Force medic cleaned my molester's brain matter off my face. I was bloody too as I tried to comprehend what I believed were my sins and transgressions. Sin was the only reason I could think of as to why God would have allowed this violation of my body and soul.

"Why did God, the supreme creator, abandon me and allow these demons to rape me? What had I done to deserve the destruction of my soul?" I wondered like countless victims before me had.

I had gone to church every week with my mother, even when my siblings and stepfather rejected God. I had witnessed sunrise Easter service at Ephesus, one of the seven churches that Paul addressed in the book of Corinthians. Sure, I fell asleep in the back pew sometimes and ran down the halls of the church "making a racket" as one of the parishioners gleefully said as she ratted me out, but I did nothing against God to warrant such a vile and evil attack. I began to hate God and religion the very moment of my attack. When they airlifted me out of the ruins of those aqueducts, all the Air Force personnel thought the zombie-like stare on my face was one of trauma, when it was one of pure hatred, anger, and contempt.

Now years later, after witnessing the attack of the young innocent girl by the pimp Dixon, my angry was renewed. My fist tightened up and I began punching the headboard of my bed until my hands were a mangled and bloody mess. I called out to God in anger and was on the verge of a blasphemous statement, when a voice in my head whispered, "I love you and will reveal Myself to you soon, but know I am with you until the end of time." I calmed down and washed and bandaged my hands in the bathroom. I lay down on my bed again, and Judge looked up, whining and whimpering. I rubbed his ears and told him that everything was going to be okay because I would be with him until the end of time. As my troubled mind recalled the earlier events that left deep emotional scars and required several years of therapy, I trembled in my bed and pulled the covers up to my chest, now covered with goosebumps. The morning light began to filter into my room at about the same time when a subconscious thought that had been deep in my memory finally surfaced. I understood that maybe, just maybe, my stepfather, the great Colonial MacGregor had something to do with my abduction and molestation. The realization that there was a connection flashed like a bolt of lightning through my mind as I drifted off to sleep.

CHAPTER 8

I slept until almost three o'clock Monday afternoon. The vibration of my cell phone on the nightstand beside the bed acted as an alarm clock, waking me up rudely. I was going to let the person on the other end know all about my displeasure when a deep bass voice greeted me, "Morning champ!" I knew it was my long-lost "papa," Mad Dog. Even though my mother died five years ago, this buffoon still wanted to hold on to a relationship that never existed. It was like my thoughts the night before had conjured up his evil spirit.

"Hey, champ. Having a big hog roast this Saturday down here at Lake Malone. I sure would like to see you. It's been a while," he said with false enthusiasm.

The conversation was so weird. It was almost like he was stalking me, trying to create a relationship that had never existed.

"Hey, Mike, how are you? I have not heard from you since you ran off and got remarried! Your wedding gift is in the mail," I said sarcastically.

"Yeah, right. I've been expecting a card, gift, or at least a phone call from you!" he grunted malignantly.

"Well, you're the only old man that runs off and gets hitched like a teenager!"

There was a long pause as though he was considering how to tactfully respond to my comment. I could sense tension on the other end of the line, but quickly he responded, "Fair enough!"

"Anyway. Like to see you and Connie next Saturday. We will do a little kayaking, and then come back and have a nice fall bonfire," he continued in an almost begging tone.

I hesitated a moment. The last thing I wanted to see was this old bastard, but then I thought that maybe he had a little money to bequeath to his stepson to make up for the lifetime of mental and emotional abuse. So perhaps it was my greed that got the better of me.

"Well, Connie and I are now divorced. Happened about a year ago. She ran off with her boss at the bank." Tactfully, I did not add that I was abusive and drunk for about eighty percent of our five-year marriage. There was a silence on the phone, and I could almost see the gears turning in Mad Dog's head. He was thinking of the most tactful way of responding. He chose to be kind, caring, and considerate.

"Sorry to hear that, champ. She seemed to be a perfect fit for you," he said with faked sympathy.

I wanted to scream into the phone and ask, "Who the fuck is this? What have you done with my stepdad, Mike?" The real Mad Dog would have been condescending and negative, probing and asking questions that were none of his damn business.

I quickly pushed my poisonous thoughts back into my subconscious. Maybe the old bastard had turned over a new leaf and was trying to make up for all the years he punished me mentally.

"Well, the bonfire starts around six, but you can come up early to kayak with me. Lake Malone is beautiful this time of year, and I have an extra boat for you," he said again in an almost pleading tone.

I began to feel sorry for the old coot. Perhaps he had mellowed in his advanced years.

"Okay, sure, I will try to make it. Can't promise anything. Goobering is very lucrative this time of year. Is it okay to bring a friend?" I said, thinking that this was my last test question.

"Sure, it will be like a double date, and you can sample Donna's home cooking. I had to make sure I got a good cook in my final years," he boasted.

Damn, if he did not pass the last test. The old Mad Dog would have asked probing questions about my friend, trying to pry into my private life. I decided to let the last remark go about the cooking. Maybe he was hinting that my departed mother was not a worthy chef when all she ever did all her life was to please him and make his pathetic life better.

"Well, thanks for the invite, Mike. I will try my best to make it, but I can't promise anything," I said in a rushed voice that sounded like I had someplace to be.

"Donna and I will be expecting you then. It will be great to see you, son." I slowly hung up the phone in shock. Did he just call me son? My dark abilities kicked in, and I knew that my dear stepfather wanted something!

I decided to take a hot shower. As soon as my feet touched the floor, Judge was staring at me with his plastic food dish lodged in his mouth as if to say, "I missed my damn breakfast. How about some lunch Rip Van Winkle?" I laughed at the comic pose of my best friend.

"Okay, coming right up, your majesty." I shuffled off to the cabinet that held the lamp chop Alpo that I was saving for a special occasion. After taking one look at my dog's pissed-off expression, I knew this indeed was that special occasion. I decided to go upstairs and check on the only two people that genuinely cared about me. After speaking with my old stepdaddy, being with Aunt Jackie and Uncle Jim would be therapeutic, like washing a bad taste out of my mouth with an ice-cold beer.

CHAPTER 9

It was almost five p.m. when I finally surfaced upstairs. I looked outside and noticed that the ice that had accumulated on the roads, grass, and the driveway had melted. I was hoping that the ice would turn to snow and that I would be snowbound and insulated in my house, safe from the demons that stalked me. Aunt Jackie was asleep on her fine leather, sectional couch, the T.V. remote still in her hand. I quietly walked around her to my Uncle Jim's situation room. I stood in front of the thick door and tentatively knocked, waiting obediently for my orders to enter the room. When I finally heard the gruff, "Get your ass in here!" I cautiously opened the door.

My Uncle Jim fancied himself as one of the best day traders in the entire universe. He often bragged about making a thousand dollars a day.

"Damn, my investment portfolio is sinking quicker than the damn *Titanic*! I want my mutual fund stocks around eight to ten percent annually, and mine are hemorrhaging around two percent. My mutual fund bonds are not doing much better at three percent," he said with his voice full of anxiety and anger.

As I sat across from him, I hesitated about what advice to give him. My financial situation was not much better than a homeless person living in a cardboard box on the streets of downtown Nashville. I was petrified that he was going to lose his fine military pension from his twenty years of service to our country for two reasons: first, it would kill him, but more importantly, I would become that homeless person living in a cardboard box on the streets of Nashville.

"Uncle Jim, the market is very volatile right now because of all the tensions in the Middle East. Oil prices are skyrocketing. Might be a good idea to sell and lie low until the crisis blows over," I said trying to sound like I had an M.B.A. in finance from Vanderbilt.

"Are you nuts? Every good trader knows that the riskier stocks during stressful times bring the best returns. It's all about R.O.I., son." I was smart enough to understand that R.O.I. was "return on investment."

"But" was all that I got out before Uncle Jim explained his new strategy.

"I am fed up with Vanguard or E-Trade. I'm going with an independent financial advisor to do my portfolio management. All my investment buddies are raving about his private investment company, and some are averaging fifteen to twenty percent return on investment even in this current turmoil."

Uncle Jim then flipped a business card with the genius's name and contact information.

"Here you go, Shaun. You may want to give him a call you poor Son of a Bitch" and then he laughed a big heart-felt chuckle. I was about to admonish him when the doorbell rang. I knew that it was my friend Pee Wee who had perfect timing. I jumped up and asked my uncle for permission to leave. It was a private joke between us.

"Permission granted, Soldier," he answered, still studying his personalized portfolio prepared by the mysterious financial advisor.

I leaped out of the chair and stuffed the business card into my pocket. I thought, "I needed to do some extensive research on this bastard. No one is going to get my butt evicted from my home. That dubious distinction belongs to my drunk ass.

A few days ago, I had invited Pee Wee over for dinner. My Aunt Jackie's lasagna was legendary in our family, and any outsider who sampled it would always inquire as to when their next invitation to consume this Italian masterpiece was to be. We were then going to drink lots of alcoholic beverages and watch Monday night football. The Indianapolis Colts were playing division rivals the Houston Texans. The teams were the Titans' two biggest arch-rivals, so abusive curse words were going to be lobbied at the officials in an exceedingly high volume. Lucky for us, the basement was soundproof. I yanked open the door and was surprised to see my buddy Pee Wee with a gorgeous blonde on his arm. She was smoking hot, with light-blue eyes and cream-colored skin, and I just knew that she had to be a hooker.

"Hey, Pee Wee. Lasagna's almost done. Guess I better tell Aunt Jackie to set another plate!" I said giving Pee Wee that "what-the-fuck?" look.

"I'm sorry, Shaun. Once she sampled some of this stuff,'" he said, indicating his body, "I couldn't get her off me. Going to start calling her static cling," Pee Wee said laughingly.

"Shaun, you know him better than that," she quickly responded. "It's the other way around. I can't get rid of this guy. He is like a damn fungus. My name is Vicki, and I hope this is not an imposition."

The goddess spoke, holding out her delicate, beautiful hand for me to shake. I gently took her hand and kissed it, saying charmingly, "Not at all, my dear. Beats looking at his ugly ass all night."

Vicki rolled her eyes and laughed with wild abandon. I liked her immediately!

After dinner, both Vicki and Pee Wee heaped mountains of praise and accolades on my aunt for such a great dinner. Vicki even offered to help my aunt with the dishes.

"Nah, that's what we have our male servant Shaun for," my uncle said, laughing like a deranged hyena. I was thoroughly embarrassed, but Aunt Jackie saved the day.

"Now, Jim, you know that you love to pull K.P. Now get your ass in there and load the dishwasher. Shaun has company. Get down there and watch some Monday night foosball, honey."

We all burst out laughing, not at my beautiful aunt saying "foosball," but at the expression on Uncle Jim's face. Nobody has ever spoken to my Uncle Jim that way except my Aunt Jackie.

We all jumped up and excused ourselves from the table while my Uncle Jim was still in a state of disbelief and shock. I slapped him on the back as I made my way to the basement door, letting him know that he was still the alpha male in the house and still had a pair. We got downstairs just in time to hear Hank Williams, Jr., ask if we were ready for some football, to which we all answered, "Hell, yes."

Since my friend had paired up with Vicki, I retrieved my date for the evening, old Johnny Walker. He was the perfect date. He kept his mouth shut and always had my back. Vicki was drinking some Amber Mist Moscato, and Pee Wee had already broken into my fridge and was helping himself to my Miller Light. Judge was so excited to have guests that he was scurrying around with his bobtail wagging back and forth at a furious pace. Judge took to Vicki immediately. He wanted her to pet him incessantly. Springer spaniels are bred to be retrievers, coveted by quail and pheasant hunters for their special abilities. Judge wanted to demonstrate his abilities to Vicki as he repeatedly made her throw his red rubber ball around the room.

After the first half, the Texans were beating the Colts by twenty points, so Pee Wee decided it was time to discuss his favorite topic, especially when he was drinking.

"Shaun, have you ever heard the Annunaki?" Pee Wee asked, his voice slurred from too many beers.

I slowly shook my head, and Vicki rolled her eyes in a dramatic fashion. I decided to humor my good friend, not wanting to embarrass him in front of his new love interest.

"No, I haven't. Would you care to enlighten me?" I requested in my most interested tone.

"Well, Shaun, they are called the shining ones, ancient astronauts from different galaxies that are responsible for building the ancient pyramids of Egypt as well as the Temple of Giza and the Sphinx. The ancient Sumerians and Egyptians did not have the engineering skills and mathematical knowledge to build those incredible landmarks. Consider that the Sphinx is over 65-feet high, and the pyramids of Giza are over 570,000 square feet and weigh over 6,000,000 tons. How did ancient people with no heavy machinery accomplish such a task?" he asked with one eyebrow comically raised.

Vicki and I looked at each other for a moment, trying to non-verbally agree as to who would offer a counterpoint, but we both shrugged our shoulders as a sign that we would surrender to Pee Wee's barrage of wild alien conspiracies. Pee Wee interpreted our silence as a sign that he would now go into a long-winded dissertation on ancient alien history.

"Well, according to Genesis 6, verses 1-4, the Annunaki are fallen angels who came to earth to have sex with humans. They would make these women their wives and would have children with them. The children would be called Nephilim--half-god and half-human. These half breeds would be giants among men. The Annunaki taught mankind astrology, witchcraft, sorcery--things God never intended man to know! The Annunaki controlled the humans and used them as slaves to mine their gold and silver. Some scholars believe that the eye on the dollar bill is the symbol of the Annunaki still watching over humans today."

Pee Wee paused long enough for Vicki to ask me if I had spiked Pee Wee's beer with some L.S.D. or other mind-expanding drug. We got a short reprieve from Pee Wee's rants when the Colts scored two touchdowns within the first five minutes of the second half. First, they marched eighty yards down the field on the strength of their rookie quarterback's arm. Then on defense, their pre-safety intercepted a Bryan Jenkins' pass on the twenty and waltzed into the endzone. Finally, it was an extremely competitive game, and if there was one thing that Pee Wee loved more than aliens, it was good football!

After an extremely exciting come-from-behind win by the Colts, Vicki turned to her date and with a straight face said, "So, let me get this straight. Demonic angel came down from heaven, had sex with all the beautiful women, and left the ugly ones alone? Then they married the beautiful ones because it was the godly thing to do, and then they had half-breed children that were giants? Finally, they built temples and pyramids to apologize to the earthmen for fornicating with their women. Is that pretty much a summary of your reasoning so far?"

I couldn't help but laugh at Vicki's comic summary of my best friend's theory because my date Johnny Walker was in complete control at this point. What really would have been shocking to Vicki was that Pee Wee was on the right track.

Pee Wee's face got a shade redder. He paused for a minute, trying not to respond too strongly to Vicki's comical version of his theory of alien interaction with humans.

"Well, my friends, do you both believe in God?" He asked the random question, preparing to defend his hypothesis. Vicki and I looked at each other and slowly nodded our heads, confirming that we did believe in God.

"Well, then, you must believe what's in the Bible!" he commented. We both again nodded that we did indeed believe the Bible, and I began to wonder where this drunken Perry Mason was heading with his line of questioning.

"Well, then, you cannot refute what the prophet Ezekiel described in chapter one. He peered into the heavens and saw a portal of pure energy, a stargate, a black hole leading to another dimension. That image is complete with four wheels within a larger wheel, inhabited by four aliens with four faces and hooves for feet. These, in my professed opinion, are early episodes of human encounters with aliens. The first of many encounters of the third kind. Actual contact with aliens that mankind has experienced throughout time."

Pee Wee paused for a brief second, not allowing for any counterpoints or questions, "In Revelation, Chapter 4, the Apostle John, while stranded on the Island of Patmos, speaks of a possible stargate, a doorway to another world that opens before him. Four beings with four faces and six wings, all covered with eyes, were seated before a spirit on a throne. Are these aliens or angels?" he asked in a quiet and drama-filled voice.

"Come on, love, the Apostle John didn't possess the words to describe what he was seeing as he peered thousands of years into the future. I have read Ezekiel 1, and I believe that cherubs or angels are holding God up on a chariot. That was quite a common image back in Biblical times. Ezekiel was incredibly detail-oriented, and he described the four beings as taking a human form. Ezekiel had a strong vocabulary and was quite capable of distinguishing between human and alien," Vicki argued all this, but in a very tactful and respectful manner. I sat back in my drunken stupor, impressed by my friend's new girlfriend's Biblical knowledge.

It was around midnight when I finally announced to the Biblical scholars that it was time to engage in verbal discourse at their own residence. I was closing the bar at around three a.m.

"You don't have to go home! You just can't stay here!" I made Pee Wee give Vicki his keys because drunk friends don't let their friends drive drunk. I hugged them both good-bye as they exited the basement door that led to the backyard. As I shut the door, I peered at my good friend Judge and asked him in a slurred voice not to repeat anything that he had heard tonight, but I could not help thinking that my overseers, the Arcturians, must have been extremely impressed with my friend's knowledge.

CHAPTER 10

For the first time in days since the aliens refused to return the body of the Nashville pimp Dixon, I slept like a baby. I had been obsessed with the thought that Nashville homicide detectives were hot on my trail and would be knocking on my door, placing me in handcuffs. I envisioned my Aunt Jackie and Uncle Jim in tears as their favorite nephew, a suspected serial killer, was led off to either prison or a nuthouse.

It was four p.m. on Tuesday afternoon, I rolled to my left, and my feet hit the floor, right in front of Judge's snout. He stirred and peered up with an expression that seemed to convene two things: "about time you got your lazy ass out of the bed," "and your feet smell like crap!" I reached down and scratched his head and apologized for awakening him from his beauty sleep. He seemed to accept my apology and scurried off to get his bowl, thinking that maybe in my state of deep regret I would fill the dish with T-bone steak or lamb chops. After feeding Judge and taking a quick shower, I hurried upstairs. I usually take Monday and Tuesdays off, but it was the beginning of winter break at Vanderbilt, and many students would need a ride to the train or airport. If I got lucky, I might even drive several students back home to their loving parents. Aunt Jackie was waiting for me at the top of the stairs, with an anxious look on her face. I gave her a big hug and thanked her for feeding my friends last night.

"Aunt Jackie, Pee Wee and his date Vicki spent the whole night raving about how good your lasagna was last night. They think you should open an Italian restaurant!" My Aunt Jackie smiled, and I felt a warm rush in my heart, knowing that I had made her day.

"Shaun, I need you to talk to your Uncle Jim. He has been cramped up in his situation room. Every time I walk by, he is cussing like a sailor."

"I definitely will, Aunt Jackie. Don't you worry your pretty, little head. You know he likes to cuss when he is day trading and things don't go exactly as he planned," I said in a very comforting tone. I smiled and gave her a reassuring hug, trying to calm her nerves. I walked back to Uncle Jim's situation room and knocked on the door. "Enter at your own peril," Uncle Jim barked. I stood there in silence as Uncle Jim was in deep concentration, preoccupied with scalping, or in laymen's terms selling his trades immediately after the trades became profitable. I looked around his office and was overwhelmed with old photographs of his platoon after their victory at Chosin Dam. The men were smiling, but the haunted look in their eyes were telltale signs of the horror of warfare.

"Can't seem to reach my price target today. I screwed up and tried to do some fading and lost my arse. I have been here since early in the morning and only made about a hundred bucks. Hell, I could make more than that by selling myself on Broadway," he said, laughing at my own joke. I thought that was a good sign because that meant his retirement pension was not in danger. I decided to create a distraction, anything to get him out of his chair.

"Uncle Jim, I need for you to ride down with me to get your prescriptions today. The pharmacist always hassles me when you're not with me."

"Sure, I will be done in a second. Tired of this chump change anyway. Can't wait to make a lot of money with my new financial advisor. I mentioned him yesterday, a damn genius my buddies are raving about. They are bragging about tremendous returns on their investments. I'm just pissed because I almost missed the boat," Uncle Jim said in a tone of mixed optimism and regret.

As we drove to the pharmacy, Uncle Jim spoke nonstop about day trading, and how he was tired of just making five or six hundred dollars a week. He mentioned that his new investor was going to manage his

investment portfolio to reap several thousand dollars a week. I asked
about this broker's background, and Uncle Jim proudly exclaimed that
his new financial advisor had an M.B.A. in finance from Vanderbilt and
had a successful career with Wanes and Briggs, a big brokerage firm in
Nashville. My ears perked up when my uncle exclaimed that the initial
investment was 200,000 dollars, which Ron, the genius, guaranteed
a twenty-five percent return on. I knew at that point Ron Mears, my
Uncle Jim's new "Golden Boy," was going to be investigated by my
Uncle Jim's personal detective service, his devoted and loyal nephew.

I dropped Uncle Jim off at his house around 5:30 and headed
toward the Vanderbilt campus. I set my destination for Nashville and
was rewarded with a customer about six miles away who at least was
heading in that direction. Goober driving is not an exact science. The
company would not give me the exact destination until I picked up
my client and started the trip on the app. It was a recent improvement
to the old app, but I still might have to wander around hell's half-acre
until I got to Vanderbilt's Campus. It was a gamble, but then everyone
knows that life is a crapshoot. I got lucky and my first client was a Vandy
student who was meeting his friends at a pub called The Library on the
corner of Alumni Drive and Broadway. The bar was cleverly named The
Library because no son or daughter liked to lie to mom and dad when
they were on a drinking binge. The name gave them cover.

For the next three hours, I drove undergrad college students to
and from Nashville's numerous bars. The tips were truly short because
everyone knows that college students are usually broke. Most students
would be enjoying their break by traveling to the Gatlinburg or
Dollywood in the Great Smoky Mountains or traveling to great hiking
spots like Falls Creek Falls or Cumming Falls off the I-40 corridor.
Unfortunately, as college students, their priority was to get drunk and
act like inebriated idiots in my Lexus, so I decided to cut my losses and
head to Nashville International Airport before one of the privileged
brats puked in my car.

I reached the airport in twenty minutes and turned into the
commercial parking lot reserved for drivers for hire. I assume my
position in the virtual waiting line which according to my app had

twenty cars in front of me. I decided to start reading a novel by John Gresham. I contemplated the fact that I would have been a great lawyer, powerful deductive reasoning capabilities, photographic memory, and charisma and charm that could win over any jury. It was almost eleven p.m. when the app squawked and commanded me to proceed to the lower terminal and pick up a customer named Ron. I hoped he was heading to Knoxville, Tennessee, about three hours away straight down I-40. That would be good money.

As I drove up to the curb, Ron was waiting for me. He is a broad-shouldered guy, with a linebacker's build, powerful and lean. His attire was extremely professional and immediately exuded extreme wealth and privilege. The silk Giorgio Armani suit that he wore suggested that he had just attended an important business meeting. He unbuttoned his suit jacket right before he entered my car. The first things I noticed about him was that his breath reeked of alcohol and the cufflinks on his shirt were diamonds, amethyst, and 14K. He was extremely drunk, and I knew that it was going to be an incredibly stressful ride. Extreme wealth, arrogance, and intoxication is a terrible combination. I told him to sit back and relax. I thought to myself if he were any more relaxed that he would be dead. I gave him my Burger King rant, and he seemed to be preoccupied or passed out. I started the trip on the app and was depressed to learn my destination was Murfreesboro, Tennessee, about thirty minutes down the road on I-24. I thought of the giant tip I might get, but then laughed to myself because first, he seemed too drunk to leave a tip, and second, wealthy bastards such as my client are so tight they can't squeeze a quarter out of their ass.

The moment the car started to roll, he opened his mouth and that moment knew that he was a candidate for an intervention.

"Sorry I'm so drunk. Needed a little liquid courage. I got a huge fear of flying but had a retiree from Arizona that just had to see me. I am Ron, and I'm running one of the biggest Ponzi schemes since Bernie Madoff. In fact, my scam is so big, I make Bernie look like a Boy Scout. There is so much fear out there about Social Security going broke that these old coots are buying my investment scam hook, line, and sinker," he said slurring his words.

I thought that he was a complete and utter idiot as I turned on the voice recorder on my surveillance system. The old saying that loose lips sink ships is true.

Ron seemed to gather his senses and calmly said that I did not have permission to record our conversation, so it was with deep regret I turned off the recording.

"All I have to do is show some investment returns and testimony from other clients, and they can't wait to sign on the dotted line. I do have a small conscience and hate taking their life savings, pensions, and various other retirement accounts, but then If I didn't fleece them, someone else would," and he laughed. The sound of his laughter sickened me as I thought of all the poor senior citizens being preyed upon by wolves and hellhounds like the piece of shit in my back seat. I hit the button on my dashboard, and the small needle inserted sleepy juice into Ron's neck. Combined with his massive alcohol consumption, the scam man was asleep within a minute.

I drove to the intervention point and backed my car into the old barn. I got out of the car very apprehensive that the old farmer would be there, waiting to fill me full of lead. I opened the car door and peered up at the full moon bathing the countryside in a silvery glow. I then had a flashback to my favorite movie as a kid as the boy rides an airborne bike into the sky with E.T. secured in the front basket, their figures silhouetted against a full moon. I knew that within five minutes Ron Mears was going to be lifted into the night air, highlighted by the same moon's silvery glow. I quickly sat next to the scam man and placed my fingers against his carotid artery. The vision almost stopped my heart, but then it began to race uncontrollably as a vision of my beloved Uncle Jim blowing his brains out with a Mossberg tactical shotgun. The terror of what I saw was compounded by the fact my Uncle Jim keeps such a shotgun in his bedroom. My mind was reeling as I tried to connect the dots! How did this slimy bastard know my Uncle Jim? Then it hit me like Mike Tyson's left jab to my jaw. This low-life bastard was the mysterious investor that my Uncle Jim had been bragging about the last couple of days! I reached back, grabbed my wallet, and searched for the business card my Uncle Jim had given me. I found the card, and my eyes focused on the picture of Ron Mears as I peered down at the scam man. Unless the bastard had a twin, I was looking at the con man that was going to swindle my cherished uncle out of his life savings.

I was consumed by the desire to race back home to check on my Uncle Jim. My head was pounding, my heart racing. I was scared to death of what I might find when I arrived. Visions of Aunt Jackie curled up to his body, blood and brain matter consuming every inch of her body raced through my mind. Most of the visions I see are future events, but could this one be an exception? Could my uncle be lying in a pool of his own blood, while I sat here alone with his drunken, soulless killer. I wanted to reach out and put my hands around this creep's neck and strangle him. Suddenly, he began to twitch and then move as I realized that I could not interfere with his fate. It would be against the laws of the universe, but more importantly, the Arcturians would be pissed.

Ron Mears's body slithered like a huge rattlesnake through the grass until he reached the point that the tractor beam lifted him gradually into the air. I watched as his body rose--up and up--toward the heavens, and then he disappeared into the clear sky, like an optical illusion. The Arcturians' craft was hidden by some cloak of invisibility as if they didn't trust me as they interfered with human destiny. It took every bit of patience in my being, to sit and wait for the Arcturians' verdict. I called my aunt's house repeatedly but got no answer, which was not strange since it was one in the morning. They turn in with the chickens. I nervously tapped the steering column like I was Keith Moon of The Who. I wanted to see the red flare shoot across the sky, meaning that scam man would not be given a reprieve, and I could race home to my Aunt Jackie and Uncle Jim.

I waited about fifteen minutes and the clone of Ron Mears appeared out of nowhere and was standing in front of my car like an apparition. Something must have gone wrong because the man was sobbing, his body hunched over in pain, his grief seeming unbearable. I was shocked, most folks that return from their intervention are giddy with excitement and optimism, but Ron Mears's reaction was the opposite. As he opened the back door, I could sense two emotions--guilt and shame. He looked like a man that had lost everything and had nothing to live for.

He then whispered, "Change of drop-off location. Could you take me to the police station? I need to purge my soul."

Even though I was in a hurry to get home and check on Uncle Jim, I said, "Sure my friend. This is the Burger King car. Have it your way."

As I drove to the police station, the man curled up into a fetal position and continued to cry like a newborn baby. I peered into my rearview mirror, hoping the depressed bastard wouldn't kill himself. I wondered how life can change in one minute. You're ready to strangle someone, and then you feel nothing but empathy and compassion.

Downtown Nashville was deserted when we arrived at the police station. I worried that Ron Mears would get mugged before he confessed to many white-collar crimes ranging from securities fraud to money laundering. As he exited my car on the way to his redemption, I wished him good luck and sincerely meant it.

I then gunned my engines and raced to my aunt's house forty miles away. I ran every stoplight, sign, and crossroads trying to get home, tears rolling down my face, knowing that I was too late to save the only father figure that I had ever known. I recklessly pulled the car into the driveway and ran around the house to the basement. I hurriedly opened the door and ran past a bewildered Judge, who in his dog brain thought he was being ignored because he chewed up my shoes a couple of nights ago. I ran up the stairs and down the hall and gently opened the door and peered in, prepared to scream in anguish.

As my eyes adjusted to the light, to my relief I saw my uncle sleeping peacefully, his chest rising and falling in a rhythmic cadence. It was the most cathartic sight I had ever witnessed. I sank to my knees, flooded with relief and for the first time in forty years thanked God for his mercy.

I went back downstairs full of gratitude and relief, patted Judge on the head, and told him in dog language that I was not mad at him, which equated to my filling his bowl with his favorite steak and lamb chops.

I soon drifted off into a troubled sleep. The last two interventions had taken a toll on my emotional health. I decided not to do any more interventions until I had a chat with John Running Bull, my mentor, and friend.

CHAPTER 11

I slept late on Tuesday morning, and as soon as my feet hit the floor, I picked up my cell phone. I hesitated before I dialed his number because I didn't want to bother an old man. I then smiled to myself, "To hell with Running Bull. He is the reason that I'm in this predicament."

He answered on the first ring. "How the hell you been doing, paleface? I thought you had been scalped!" his laughter sounded like a wolf's howl wild and untamed.

"I'm fine, my friend. Thanks for your concern. I'm just stressed out. Need your wisdom and guidance. The last two intervention have been tough on my heart. I need to meet with you as soon as possible."

I hated the sound of my needy, pleading voice. There was a slight pause. Then the Navajo medicine man spoke, "You are the last of the soul searchers on earth, and it is my privilege and honor to counsel you. Besides if you screw up the entire planet is doomed. I will meet with you at our regular spot. How about three p.m.?"

"I will see you then, John, and thank you." I smiled and a wave of relief swept over my body.

I was not only concerned about my last two interventions but was also genuinely concerned about the mysterious invitation from my stepfather. According to my cell phone, it was about 1:30 in the afternoon. Knowing that it would take me about an hour to drive to my meeting with John, I hopped in the shower and tried to wash the cobwebs out of my mind. Despite the hot water running down my face

I could not shake a feeling of impending doom, as if great storm clouds were gathering in the distance, laden with violence and extreme cruelty.

I fed Judge and checked on my Uncle Jim, sound asleep in his recliner and snoring slightly, his large chest rising and falling in a rhythmic cadence. I glanced at his peaceful face and made a mental note to make sure he knew of Ron Mears's treachery. I found Aunt Jackie cleaning like a possessed Irish banshee. I kissed her on the cheek explaining that I was going to meet an old friend, knowing that she would have no idea where I went an hour later. I suddenly felt great pity for her and bent down and kissed her forehead. I gently told her that I loved her.

I left the house feeling a sense of guilt and shame. Was I putting their lives in danger? I knew my relationship with the Arcturians could be as dangerous as cancer or heart disease. I back my car out of the driveway, toying with the idea of telling Running Bull that Ron Mears would be my last intervention.

As I drove to meet Running Bull, my thoughts went back in time, and I began to reflect upon our first meeting and the great impact that the John Running Bull had made on my life. Two years ago, I picked him up at The Warpath, a favorite drinking hole for Native American Indians in South Nashville. The name itself hints to the great residual anger and resentment the indigenous people felt against the invader, white man. He was waiting for me on the street corner, dressed in worn-out wrangler jeans and a bright red flannel shirt. He had a black vest made of leather and a large black hat with a beaded band that had Navajo insignia encircling the top. He also wore a belt made of animal skins, and his blue jeans were tucked neatly into beaded-hide leather moccasins. The moccasins had a colorful emblem of a bald eagle on the tip. He had exceedingly high cheekbones, and a scar ran from one of the cheek bones down to his mouth. His bronzed skin had the texture of worn leather. His long jet-black hair was tied in a ponytail and flowed down his back like a serpent. His most notable feature was his eyes. They were extremely dark but were like embers of energy and vitality. A magical quality of charisma and strength exuded from them. I thought about how first impressions were so important for character assessment, and the first thought that popped into my head was that this was a man who was extremely proud of his heritage and would fight to the death to protect his people.

On that fateful day he got in my car, and I let him have the Burger King rant. He laughed and spoke, his voice echoing from the back seat like he was on a high mountaintop speaking down to me,

"Well, paleface, if I had it my way, I would command that you blue-eyed, fork-tongue white bastards would give us back our land."

I was shocked and knew that this trip was going to be extremely uncomfortable.

Then he laughed, and his laughter sounded like a war cry.

"Just screwing with ya, Shaun. I am glad to meet you. I am John Running Bull, and you are my new friend, the last soul searcher on earth."

I thought that this crazy Indian had consumed too much fire water, but over the next two months as I got to know him well, John Running Bull would convince me that I, Shaun MacGregor, was indeed the last of my species. On the first trip Running Bull explained that he had been a code talker for the United States Marine Corps during World War II and was proud of his service. His native tongue, Navajo, related to Apache, could not be broken by the Germans or Japanese. Before the Indian languages were used in code, Germans intercepted many Allied transmissions and were able to wreak havoc on many "secret operations," causing massive loss of life. Supply lines and troop movements were routinely bombed by Messerschmitts that came screaming out of the clouds.

"Yep, we were the special ones, praised in public by our superiors, but hated for our skin color," John said with a deep sadness in his voice. As I dropped him off at his run-down apartment, he mentioned that he wanted me to be his private driver and that he would pay me cash whenever he needed me.

"Listen I will tip you well and pay you three times what Goober pays. Please give me your number, and I will call you twenty-four hours before I need you," he said as he pulled a one-hundred-dollar bill out of his wallet. I shook my head, in a non-compliant manner. I simply could not take that much of a tip from a World War II veteran. Even this drunk has a sense of right and wrong.

He finally convinced me to take the Benjamin, by refusing to get out of my car until I relented. We exchanged phone numbers, and that's how John Running Bull would become my mentor and number one customer. Most of all, he would be my friend. Little did either of us realize that our bond would be greater than brothers, and that our commitment to saving humanity would be the greatest achievement of our lives.

CHAPTER 12

We met at a rundown diner near Broadway. John was sitting at a table near the men's room, his back against the wall. He was positioned in such a way that any motion or movement was quickly scanned by his eagle eyes and processed through his warrior brain as either friendly or threatening action. A big grin spread across his face as I came through the door.

"Why didn't you call me to come pick you up? I always give my best customer a freebie once a month," I laughed.

"I decided that a mile walk would be good for me, a little cardio never hurt anyone. After all, the heart bypasses need to be walked at least one a day, like my dog," he smiled.

"How is Running Dog these days? Why are we meeting here? The food stinks," I commented in a slightly bewildered tone.

"Running Dog is doing fine. But the damn Doberman eats so much he is about to eat through my meager social security. I am scared not to feed him, however. Afraid I might go to the afterlife as dog poo," His laughter echoed off the diner walls.

"Besides the coffee is great, and there are certain fringe benefits," the chief said as he eyed the beautiful dark-skinned beauty who routinely waited on us. He then winked at the younger women and waved her over to the table.

"Hello, my little Pocahontas." Then he broke off into their native tongue and said some things that made the younger women blush and then laugh. I wished I could crawl under the table and just ordered my regular plate of meatloaf and mashed potatoes.

"John, how did you find one of the few Navajo waitresses in Nashville?" I asked with astonishment.

"Simple! She is the daughter of one of my friends at the American Legion, a fellow veteran from the war," he explained with not one ounce of shame or guilt.

"You're a filthy old man. You are twice her age, and she's the daughter of one of your friends. Have you no shame?" I asked with a broad smile on my face.

"Ah, Shaun, when you get my age! She and I both know that I'm harmless! My totem pole even though it's made of wood has been in hibernation for years!" The bravest, best human I had ever known laughed with all his heart and massive soul.

After we finished eating, I looked him dead in the eye, and said, "I can't do this anymore. I know the Arcturians need me to be their earthly liaison, but these interventions are taking a toll on my fragile mental health, barely on life support with the help of Johnny Walker. You told me that my intervening in these people's lives was saving humanity. I just can't see that. There are billions of people on earth. How does getting rid of one pimp stop all the pedophiles, rapists, and murders on earth?" I tried to keep the anger and frustration out of my voice.

John Running Bull stared at me, trying to read my body language, trying to determine whether I was serious.

"Ah, Shaun, your race always underestimates the interconnectedness of life, how everything in the natural world including human lives is interwoven. "Have you ever seen a movie called *Final Destination*? The movie explains the concept of interconnectedness, showing that events and situations can alter future events," he explained staring in the distance as if he were reading from a movie script. The Arcturians, who have been with mankind for thousands of years, know which lives need an intervention to save mankind from disastrous events.

"Huh, come again," I quipped, giving him a look of non-comprehension, kind of the way Judge looks at me when he was trying to understand human instructions.

"Remember when you told me of the man who burst into the black church bent on committing mass murder? What if one of the parishioners might have been killed if you hadn't intervened. What if he was a medical researcher that later would find a cure for cancer, A.I.D.S., or some damn virus that would kill millions of people? Your actions saved millions of lives that day, Shaun. That shark investor Ron Mears. You told me he was going to milk your uncle of thousands of dollars. He had several hundred customers, Shaun. What if one of his clients had millions of dollars and was going to donate a vast fortune to a third-world country to delay starvation and famine after crops had failed because of global warming? Your actions that day would have saved millions of innocent lives, Shaun."

John Running Bull, then like a great salesman, shut his mouth and gave me time to assimilate the wisdom he had shared.

"That's just fate," I said knowing it was a weak defense.

"Ah, Shaun, after our trip to Sedona, you know better than that. The Great Spirit only benefits mankind. He has no wish to punish mankind, even though we deserve it. These are actions of the demons of the underworld trying to destroy people or of the Annunaki, the evil star people trying to control and manipulate humans for their own selfish desires and profits."

John concluded the conversation by folding his hands. He knew that he had convinced me to continue my commitment to the Arcturians.

"So, the Arcturians know that my actions each and every time will save millions of lives?" I asked already knowing the answer. The great chief nodded his head yes.

On to the next order of business. I told John about the mysterious call from my stepfather and his invitation to attend a barbecue at his home near Lake Malone.

"I can't help to think that he is stalking me, trying to find out information about my current life. I think he knows of my link to the Arcturians," I said nervously playing with the fork in front of me.

The chief fished into his pocket and brought out a miniature listening device like the ones private detectives use to record cheating spouses or someone hiring a hitman. The device looked like a mobile phone charger, complete with a S.I.M. card.

"I want you to take his phone charger and link the S.I.M. card number to your phone. When you dial the card number, you can listen to conversations on your cell phone from anywhere in the world," John said in a hushed tone as though he was a covert operative for the government.

I picked up the device. it looked like a regular phone charger you plug into the wall.

"Why?" I asked, perplexed by such a severe reaction from John.

He looked me dead in the eyes, and calmly said, "I believe that your father is a spy for the Annunaki." John got up to leave.

"So, you're going to drop a bomb on me like that and then get up and leave," I said indignantly.

He shook my hand and explained that I needed to be alone to process the shocking news. As he walked by me, he patted my shoulder and told me to call him after I visited my stepfather. He has gone like a specter in one of my nightmares. Two things occurred to me as I stood there in that busy diner. John was genuinely concerned about my stepfather's contacting me, about my personal safety. The second thing that sank in was that my stepfather was a frigging alien.

CHAPTER 13

As I drove home from the restaurant, I began to reflect on the events leading up to my encounter with the Arcturians on Devil's Bridge in Sedona, Arizona. Over the next several weeks, John Running Bull would speak of the Navajo tribes of New Mexico, Arizona, and Utah, repeating encounters with the Anasazi or the star people, their many encounters depicted in petroglyphs in the subterranean caves in southwest Utah. John's father, a respected elder and medicine man, claimed to have been abducted many times by the star people and claimed that they instructed him in medical knowledge and interventional techniques that he used to save many lives among his people.

I would listen to his mumbo jumbo for weeks because of his generous tips. Hell, if I could listen to my ex-wives recap of their favorite daytime soap operas, I could listen to this old man's stories of lame-ass star people. He also spoke of my gift, the ability to soul search another human being with the touch of my hand. I told him that I have touched many women on dates or in bars and never felt anything but a vicious slap across my face. He laughed and told me that I wasn't touching them in the right place. I proudly retorted that it felt right to me.

I will never forget the day that he turned me into a true believer of his impossible claims. I had picked him up around five p.m. He had called me twenty-four hours in advance and wanted me to take him to his favorite restaurant for dinner. It was a place called The Blue Taco-- obviously a Mexican joint--that specializes in seafood fajitas.

On that day, I pulled over to the curb, and he greeted me, with his regular, "How are you doing, paleface?" to which I quickly retorted, "Not bad you old worn-out redskin." We both roared with laughter. It was our way of bonding.

As soon as he got in my car, he told me to pull into the vacant lot next to his apartment. I was very leery because I had seen drug addicts expressing the freedom to use in broad daylight at that same place. I didn't want their expended needles to puncture my new Goodyear tires. I cautiously pulled into the parking lot. As soon as I did, he grabbed my hand with the strength of a wrestler. He placed my hand on his carotid artery. Immediately, I recoiled with the clarity of the vision of my friend being held down. A man in a marine dress uniform cut his face with a switchblade knife.

The marine was laughing as the cut was made, and I heard him say, "This is for all my ancestors that your people scalped." John then removed my hand, and I understood the potential of my gift to see into the past or to future lives of those that I touch, depending on what the Arcturians wanted me to see. I felt three powerful emotions for having such a remarkable gift, as well as pity and empathy for my friend who had served his country with great distinction yet was betrayed by his brother in arms.

I looked at him with sadness and asked, "So what now, my friend?"

He looked at me with a renewed sense of hope and enthusiasm, knowing that he had finally convinced me of my powers. He triumphally said, "We are traveling to Sedona, Arizona, to meet your brethren and fulfill your destiny!"

I thought, "What the hell! A free vacation to a place I have never been before."

Also, Aunt Jackie and Uncle Jim needed a break from my ugly mug.

We landed in Phoenix, Arizona, and rented a Ford Tundra for the last leg of our journey of about two hours to Sedona, the undisputed champion of the most U.F.O. sightings on the planet.

While John drove, I was amazed at the vegetation that survived in this dry, arid climate, not only numerous cacti but desert anemone and hibiscus. The next sunrise watched us passively as we drove on.

I looked toward the horizon and could almost see my favorite actor, John Wayne, chased by Apache warriors on chestnut-colored Mustangs, the Superstition Mountains in the background. I noticed the scarcity of water and realized what a precious natural resource it is.

As though he read my thoughts, John mumbled as if he was in a trance, "The star people left thousands of years ago, giving mankind instructions on how to preserve our Mother Earth, but greed has led to Gulf oil spills, pipeline failures in pristine wetlands, and carbon emissions from hydraulic fracturing. These actions have made Mother Earth sick, and I fear that the Arcturians will not return until we heal this planet."

He continued, "I believe the Annunaki are in complete power and controlling the destruction of the Earth's biosphere and atmosphere including the ozone layer."

I looked at him, and asked the obvious question, "Why would that be the case?"

"The Annunaki are planning an invasion, not a direct assault. They are trying to turn the environment into a toxic wasteland unfit for human life, he said with a slight shrug of his shoulders.

"Why would they do that?" I asked, feeling like a slow third-grade student.

"The Annunaki are genetically unable to survive on earth because the oxygen we breath is like poison to them, so they are slowly changing the planet, increasing emissions of carbon dioxide and carbon monoxide, which is the ideal mixture of gases for their survival," John replied in a hushed, yet serious tone.

I looked at him with a mixture of fear and trepidation and wondered if my new friend had taken too long a puff on the proverbial peace pipe.

We arrived in Sedona around one in the afternoon. I was amazed by the steep red-rock canyon ablaze in a golden hue with the afternoon sun. The steep canyon walls eventually creeped down to a pine forest.

Suddenly, I felt a deep spiritual charge and a genuine feeling of well-being that spread throughout my entire body.

I glanced at John who said, "People travel from around the globe to hear the muted thunder that seems to originate from the rocks.

Special energies called vortexes are omnipresent in the area and seem to be an interdimensional portal to an alternate galaxy. In fact, many believe that's why there have been so many reports of U.F.O.s in the area, aliens seemed to be attracted to this sacred area. The portals are like an airport, many different travel destinations in a centralized hub."

I looked around and noticed New Age culture was alive and well in the Sedona area, stores selling everything from herbal remedies for cancer to hypertension lined the streets. I saw several tourists entering shops specializing in healing and hypnotherapy, spas where folks can get in touch with their inner being through yoga or meditation. I also noticed a shop that offered psychic readings done by spiritual guides. Sedona's inhabitants were cashing in on the metaphysical aura of this special place.

John took me on a tour of the area--to Boynton Canyon, Slide Rock State Park, Cathedral Rock and finally Bell Rock. The sun was setting when John said we need to get some rest.

I quickly asked, "Why?" like a moron stuck on that one-word question.

Tonight, under a full moon, we will travel to Devil's Arch, a 50-foot-tall and 40- foot-wide sandstone arch," he said in a mysteriously ominous tone.

"Why?" I asked, unable to stop myself.

"Shaun, tonight your new life will begin. Your soul will be energized, and your life's purpose will be defined, my friend. Tonight, you have a job interview with those that have protected humankind from extinction for eons." He then winked at me, and I felt a tingle of excitement and fear course through me at the same time.

Now I gripped the steering column of my Lexus, as my mind receded in time to that fateful day almost two years ago. I was concentrating on the curving backcountry road to Highway 431 right outside of Adairsville, Kentucky, and trying to focus on that night that changed my destiny forever. There was something from that night in Sedona lurking on my subconscious mind, something that had ramifications for my current life.

In Sedona, we stayed at a very secluded old motel about 10 miles out of town, a low-budget, cockroach-infested place cleverly named The Getaway Galaxy Inn.

The motel was built in the fifties and had been newly renovated, but no amount of renovation could remove the musty smell and traces of mold on the ceiling. The room contained two double beds, both covered with bedspreads that had images of U.F.O.s sewn into the fabric. The wallpaper in the room was colorful and depicted characters from old movies of alien encounters and invasions, scenes from movies like H.G. Wells' *War of the Worlds* or from *The Body Snatchers* were plastered everywhere.

I was sound asleep, when John kicked my foot, which was hanging off the mattress, so I guess John thought that kicking my foot was the best way to get my adrenaline flowing.

"Get up, sleeping beauty," he quipped as he handed me a Taurus 12-shot automatic pistol before my feet hit the floor.

"What the Hell is that for?" I asked, still trying to shake the cobwebs from my sleepy head.

I remember him saying, "It's for the beasts that you may encounter during our four-mile hike to Devil's Arch. We are traveling during the hour when spirits of the underworld mix with the living" His voice sounded out of this world.

I sat there for a moment, trying to comprehend his words. It would have appeased me if he had said we would encounter bears, coyotes, or mountain lions, real nocturnal creatures that own the night. I could have dealt with that fine, but when he spoke of the undead and supernatural entities roaming the night, my pulse quickened, and my hand involuntarily trembled.

John noticed that and calmly said," Ah, paleface, don't worry. The Arcturians will protect you!"

Scared of the visions and emotions that had come with my recalling that mysterious and dangerous night, I tightened my grip on the steering column and decided to pull off the road.

Visions of the past continued. I remembered John driving without his headlights on a back road leading to Devil's Arch and to our encounter with the star people called the Arcturians.

John had weird night vision. He could see at night like some wild animal hunting its prey. I began to feel extremely paranoid about my friend. "What if he was a serial killer and had lured me out here and was going to make some weird sacrifice to the aliens of his psychosis? I felt for my nine millimeter tucked securely in my jeans and chastised myself, "Why would he give me a gun if he were going to slaughter me?" I then bit my lip. "Hell, I didn't even check to see if the dam gun he had given me was loaded!

We finally arrived at the end of the dirt road, and John backed the Ford Tundra up into a getaway position. I exited the vehicle and could see Devil's Arch about 2,000 feet above me. The moon had bathed it in a silvery light, and I marveled at the natural beauty of my surroundings. John got out and handed me some night vision goggles, and I noticed that he was now packing a Mossberg tactical shotgun. I didn't know whether to feel relieved by this or alarmed knowing that I had a measly nine millimeter, probably unloaded.

We started our ascent to Devil's Arch, the landscape now awash in the weird glow of the night vision goggles. I looked up to see several shooting stars streaking across the sky and silently wondered if it was the Archturians' spacecraft on its way to our rendezvous. The chill in the air--or fear itself--made me shiver. My central nervous system was on high alert. John was ten feet in front of me, not even breathing hard after 1.000 feet of climbing.

Suddenly a huge mountain lion emerged from behind a boulder directly behind me. I swung around but was too late. it pounced, and I could see its claws protruding ready to slice me in two. I didn't even have time to scream. At that instance, I thought that my time on earth was over. I was frozen in fear. Then to my amazement the beast seems to hit a brick wall and harmlessly fall to the ground two feet from me. I then watched in amazement as it vanished into thin air.

John then whirled around, and said with no emotion, "The Arcturians' force field is some pretty crazy shit, huh?"

We finally reached the summit. I stood on a very narrow strip of ground spanning the gorge connecting two separate canyon walls. If I stepped ten feet left or right, I would be freefalling to my death 2,000 feet below. I was amazed by the surrounding topography as it unfolded in front of me. Even awash in the strange green glow of my night vision goggles, it was beautiful. I was completely and utterly in a state of euphoria and awe, and one emotion spread throughout my body-- complete and utter peace.

Suddenly the ground beneath me began to vibrate. I panicked knowing that the vibration was going to knock me off my perch and send me to my premature death. I could feel myself falling and looked around for John, but he had disappeared. My night vision goggles were swept off my face, and I was in a spinning vortex or tunnel of light.

It was like a spinning rainbow, glowing with colors that I couldn't have imagined. I was falling at an incredible speed, and suddenly I stopped, suspended in the air. I closed my eyes, wishing and hoping that when I opened them, I would be standing on the arch, calming peering at the night sky.

Before I could open my eyes, I felt a presence. I knew that John was standing right beside me, so I opened them hoping to see his ugly Navajo face but when I did, I was horrified to be surrounded by giant, shiny beings. They were about ten feet tall, with a humanoid form. They had an elongated form with stringy arms and legs. Each foot and hand had ten appendages. They had huge craniums with a large oval-shaped eye in the middle of their foreheads. My first vision was blurry because I was blinded by their brightness, but my eyes slowly focused and I could see them clearly. It was as if they were fine tuning my eyes, so I could see them. They had encircled me and were chanting something in a high-pitched tone.

The largest one broke free of the others and floated toward me. It reached out and touched my forehead. I almost fainted with fear. It began to telepathically communicate with me. The shining being said, "Have no fear! You are among your brethren."

The being went on to explain that the Arcturians have been helping mankind survive for centuries, protecting them from the violence of the

Annunaki. It seems that they had broken from the Annunaki several thousand years ago, much like the pilgrims breaking away from the overbearing Church of England. They were fallen angels but wanted to protect mankind after the Annunaki vowed to terminate us. The Annunaki had sent wars, famine, and even viruses to punish humans.

The Shining One then stroked my face, almost like a parent would caress a child. The being told me that I was the last Soul Searcher on Earth, because the Annunaki murdered your entire Lineage. I was to act as their liaison, performing actions on earth that would stop the Annunaki. The being then did something that caught me by complete surprise. It wrapped its long arms around me. At first, I thought it was going to consume me like a tasty morsel, but then I felt the love that was like nothing I had ever felt. It was burning through my soul, like a flame that would consume paper or a dry virgin forest leaving everything pristine and perfect. I closed my eyes and tears flowed down my face, knowing that I was in a sense home after years of wandering. I stood there with my arms around the identity feeling complete peace, but then something was wrong. I no longer felt its presence. I opened my eye, to see the look of complete and utter alarm and concern on John's face.

"Hey, Shaun. You okay? If you don't die, I will never talk shit to you again," John said as he held me in his arms. He was kneeling over me, rocking me back and forth.

"Get the hell off me, dude" I shouted thinking that John, being the old pervert that we had joked about, was trying to sodomize me. He finally let me go and looked at me with a look of complete and utter shock,

"Dude, you passed out. Your eyes rolled back in your head and then you died. You stopped breathing and had no pulse for almost 10 minutes," he said looking at me like I was a ghost or a spirit from the underworld.

"I am so glad you are alive, paleface. How am I going to get your ass off this arch in the middle of the night? I then thought about throwing your body off the arch, telling everyone you accidently fell," he laughed, asking me if I remembered anything while I was passed out.

I then winked at him and whispered, "Chill out, John, I just went to a little family reunion."

I will never forget the look on his face when he comprehended the fact that I finally knew who or what I was.

Like being in a trance, I was suddenly only ten minutes from home. I was driving my Lexus on automatic pilot, physically driving, but my mind and soul were still in Sedona.

I arrived home around 6:30 p.m. and found Uncle Jim in front of the tube watching the local news. I sat down beside him, and suddenly Ron Mears' face appeared on the screen, and the news dude droned on about how Mears had cheated several hundred retirees out of their life savings. The anchor explained how Mears had run a Ponzi scheme that made Bernie Madoff's scam look like child's play.

"Well, I will be damned! That crooked bastard! I guess I escaped a bullet," my uncle said with a sigh of relief. I am so glad he could not read my mind, for he would have been shocked to learn that it was more like a shot-gun shell he had escaped, his own shell.

CHAPTER 14

I decided to take the next week off. The upcoming weekend was the big cookout at my alien stepfather's crib, and I wanted to be rested and relaxed for that traumatic experience. I woke around ten a.m. on Wednesday morning. It was the 18th of October, and my stepfather's cookout was three days away. I was startled as I heard a loud knock at my backdoor. Judge, who had been sleeping on the bear skin rug next to my bed, let out a low-pitched bark and made a beeline to the door. I just knew it was a Nashville detective coming to arrest me for the disappearance of Brian Dixon.

I got out of the bed and hurried to the door, petrified that Judge would devour the detective, thus making me a suspect in two murders. I opened the door.

Pee Wee and Vicki were standing there with matching flannel shirts, jeans, and hiking boots, like Bobbsey twins.

"Let's go hiking, dude. Vickie and I are going to Albany, Kentucky to check out Seventy Six Falls. Get your damn walking stick and boots, you old fart."

Pee Wee wanted to include me for two reasons, He knew that I was in a major depression over the breakup with my third wife, and that I was crazy about hiking in the fall. I didn't want to be a third wheel and was going to deprive them of my presence, but then I looked at Vicki. The radiance of her smile and her beautiful eyes pierced my soul-- or to put in caveman terms her appearance made me quite horny. It had been almost three months since I touched a woman, and I was wallowing in self-pity.

I ushered them into the house. Judge was so glad to see his new friend Vicki that he was rubbing up against her like she was his new love interest, and I couldn't blame him. If it weren't for her dating my best friend, I would have been romancing her like a modern-day Romeo.

"Sure, I will chaperone you all. Protect you from all the wild beasts. Be your trail guide, making sure you don't get lost."

"Let me change into a matching flannel shirt, so we can look like some weird triplets on the trail," I said laughing. Pee Wee and Vicki waited for me in the living room, with Judge curled up next to Vicki. As I was getting dressed, I reflected on how bad I needed this hike because hiking had always been therapeutic for me. There is something almost Zen-like about leaves crackling under my hiking boots, the fall sun caressing my body like a long-lost lover, and the coolness of the air stimulating and energizing my body to press its physical limits.

We loaded into Pee Wee's Jeep Cherokee. Pee Wee and I rode in the front, while Vicki and Judge rode in the back seat. Judge was resting his head on Vickie's lap, his eyes bright with excitement, ecstatic to tag along with the humans.

"Did you know that Lake Cumberland is 100 miles long and runs through six counties in Kentucky? The source of Seventy Six Falls is Indian Creek. It meanders over an 80-foot cliff, and empties into Cumberland Lake. The cove near the waterfalls is party central to many boaters in the summer when it is populated by pontoons, house- and speedboats from dawn to dusk. Many drunken sailors climb the cliff to the falls and jump off. That's why at the tourist overlook, three or four crosses can be seen. I guess it's a way of communicating to the drunken idiots that they died in a drunken state, the crosses trying to direct their souls to somewhere other than hell for eternity," Pee Wee concluded like a Baptist preacher.

"Pee Wee, how in the hell do you know that jumpers who perish will end up in hell?" I asked, knowing that I will be thoroughly entertained by his answer.

"Says in the good book that a camel has a better chance of passing through the eye of a needle than drunks or a rich man going to heaven," Pee Wee said triumphantly.

I laughed until I farted, "Damn, man, you must have been drunk, when you read that passage because it doesn't say a damn thing about drunks." I then gave my friend a slight jab to his elbow because he was such a dumbass.

"Pee Wee, you sure know a lot about these falls. I thought you have never been there?" Vicki chimed in from the backseat, playfully smacking him on the back of his huge head.

"Unlike some people in this jeep, I read, my dear found an article about this place online on a website that catered to tourists visiting the Bluegrass State," Pee Wee replied.

During our two-hour trip, I discovered that Vicki was a registered nurse at Vanderbilt Hospital. Shame on me for thinking that she worked in a topless bar! I deeply respected nurses because they are like angels going the extra mile for strangers, caring for them better than their own families. She even worked with heart patients in a catherization lab, dealing with folks that needed stents or other lifesaving interventions on the most important muscle in the body. Since I was the poster child for heart disease, I felt an immediate sense of attraction and admiration for her. I wondered how Pee Wee, an assistant manager at a small grocery store, had been paired with such a beautiful, amazing woman. I guess the statement that God watches out for drunks and fools is accurate because my best friend qualifies in both categories. At that very moment in the recesses of my evil brain, I knew that I would betray my best friend by seducing his girlfriend and start in motion a plan that would ultimately cost my best friend his life.

October 18th was a beautiful but chilly fall day, one perfect for hiking. The colors of the trees were incredible. The sugar maples were a brilliant shade of gold, and the oak trees, not to be undone, were a deep shade of crimson red. The kaleidoscope of colors made my damaged heart leap in my chest and slowly arrested my depression.

"October is dressed up and playing her tune," I said, making a reference to the famous song by Seals and Croft.

Pee Wee just had to correct me, being the know it all that he was: "I believe that if you're making a reference to the classic song summer breeze, the month that is dressed up and playing her tune is July." He looked in the mirror seeking Vicki's praise for his great intelligence.

"Oh, Pee Wee, don't be so anal. This is not *Jeopardy*, and frankly, I like Shaun's comparison because October is a much more colorful month. July's outfit is too dull and boring."

I was immediately further smitten with this woman; she was killing me softly with her presence.

We finally made it to the waterfalls and parked our car in the parking lot above Indian Creek, the source water for the 80-foot phenomena. We piled out of the car like third graders on a field trip. I breathed in the fresh air, knowing this day was going to wash the last three interventions from thoughts. Judge bounded out of the car, and I immediately put a leash on him because if I didn't, he would be in the local newspaper as the only dog to jump from Cumberland Falls. My canine friend had not one morsel of fear in his shaggy body. We hiked some stairs to the side of the falls to an overlook slightly above them. As we reached the top, there was a conclave area with a stone wall that acted as a resting, viewing area. The view that assaulted my vision was a spectacular cove filled with blueish-green water and large red-rock cliffs reaching for the clear, crystal blue skies. On the cliff, there was a three-story A-framed home built on pilings. The home looked like a large cabin built with supreme pine and cedar. The large bay windows faced the cove, and I could only imagine the view that such a piece of paradise would offer.

"Can't see the dam falls!" Pee Wee said in an anguish tone. I then noticed a trail leading away from the overview and mentioned that the trail might lead to an area along the lake's edge that would offer better viewing of the falls. Pee Wee took the bait, and he and Vicki started down the dirt path. He turned, not wanting to leave me alone in my fragile state, fearing that I might take a final plunge into the cool waters of the Cumberland.

"Do you want to come along?" he asked.

"No, but I think Judge might want to tag along," I said knowing that the dog would protect them from any wild beast that might stalk them, but more importantly Judge would run up the trail to alert me if Pee Wee adventurously fell into the lake. I also suspected that my friend wanted to be alone with his charming lady, and then the part of my brain controlled by the bad thought, "Better enjoy your last days with her because soon she will be mine!"

When they were gone, I meditated on the surroundings. The reflection of the brilliant colors of fall foliage seemed to cast a vision of a lake on fire. For some reason my mind returned to the anger, guilt, and fear I felt after my sexual abuse. I was damaged goods, never to feel comfortable in my own skin, thinking that maybe my sinful nature had brought down negative karma upon me forever.

As a younger man, I was so angry that I fantasized about tracking down pedophiles and slaughtering them one by one. I had watched so many crimes show that I knew that repetition would get you apprehended, so I would vary my modus operandi. I would pick different geographic areas and use different weapons, appearing to strike at random. I would leave no forensic evidence behind--no DNA, no fingerprints, no shoe prints. I would have no credit card purchases along the route. Everything from hotel rooms, car rentals, and gas would be paid for with cash. I would be dubbed the ghost killer because I would do my deed and vanish into thin air. I would always create an alibi. I would also have travel arrangements out of the country in case I should need them. In the Bible it says vengeance is the Lord's. That might be true, but I was going to be the instrument he used to set up the meeting between Him and the demons in human camouflage that committed these hideous acts on children. I was almost ready to start my killing when I thought better of it. I had a girlfriend who was a school counselor with a degree in psychology, a deeply religious woman who loved God with every fiber of her being. One night I told her of my desire to be a serial killer, and she said that I would perish in a lake of fire.

"Why would a loving God allow my soul to be destroyed?"

She looked at me with great passion and said, "Shaun, maybe God loves you very much, and even though it caused him great anguish, he allowed those men to attack you because that's where your ministry would lie--helping those inflicted with the curse of sexual abuse. He knows you had to experience such pain to minister to others that have been molested or raped. He has chosen you to be a vessel of righteousness and hope for thousands of his children. You are his warrior, his soldier through your intervention. You will bring glory to his kingdom by saving his most precious ones, his little children." She uttered these words with tears flowing down her cheeks. I began to weep, and she rocked me back and forth like I was a baby, while softly praying for my salvation.

I would have married that sweet saint, but two days later she was killed in a terrible automobile accident. Tears flowed down my cheeks, as I thought of my possible redemptress and angel.

I was staring at the lake of fire when Vicki spotted me sitting on the bench, weeping silently. I thought that she would think me unmanly for such an exhibition of emotion, but the look on her face conveyed two emotions--compassion and empathy. I then knew at that moment that she was my soulmate and the woman that would replace my angel from years ago.

"Damn, Shaun, you missed it, buddy. What an awesome view of the falls!" Pee Wee said in an excited tone.

I just sat there staring at the lake of fire and the top of the falls, watching the water cascade over the edge of the cliff. I never suspected that less than a month later Vicki and I would be leaping off the ledge of the waterfalls hand in hand.

CHAPTER 15

I woke up Thursday morning totally obsessed with my new love interest--the very sexy, beautiful nurse named Vicki. I chastised myself for being fixated with my best friend's girl, but I am an obsessive compulsive, bi-polar individual so once someone or something gets in my head, I have no control over it. I would invite Pee Wee and Vicki over to watch Thursday night football and eat more of Aunt Jacki's lasagna, an offer that neither Vicki nor Pee Wee would turn down. I said to myself that I would have that beautiful vixen by the end of the night.

I patted Judge's head, feeling good about my diabolical plan. Judge cocked his head to one side as if to say, "Shame on you for betraying your best friend."

I went upstairs and asked Aunt Jackie if she would cook up some more lasagna for my friends, and she replied that it would be an honor to serve her special dish to my good friends, never suspecting that I had just made her an accomplice to my wicked plan. Uncle Jim was so happy not to have made a financial mistake, he patted my leg as I walked by and said, "Shaun, you gave me such sound, logical advice the other day that I'm going to give you a raise."

"Thanks, Uncle Jim, that means a lot to me," I said, not realizing I was being set up.

"Yes, sir, I am going to let you stay here for free and all meals are on me," his laughter echoed off the ceiling.

I laughed and quickly replied, "Yes, Sir, Master, appreciate your kindness."

I was reading the local paper, when Pee Wee and Vicki knocked on the door, and I almost ran to the door in sweet anticipation of seeing the object of my desire. Pee Wee was decked out in his Green Bay Jersey and matching green jeans, while Vicki had a floral V-neck sweater on, which showed her ample bosoms. I almost passed out with desire.

"Packers going to kick some Cowboy ass today," Pee Wee bellowed as he walked into the house, startling my Uncle Jim out of a deep sleep. He sat up in his chair and yelled, "Incoming, everyone take cover!" He then fell back in his chair fast asleep. I told Pee Wee several times to keep the noise down because my Uncle suffered from P.T.S.D. from his time in the Marine Corps.

"Damn, Pee Wee, why do you always have to be so loud?" I asked angrily, and then I thought about my covert operation of stealing his women and calmed down.

My friend blushed and apologized, and he quickly changed the subject and his tone whispering, "So, is the lasagna done?" For some reason, his comical response made Vicky and me laugh quietly until our sides split. After a great meal, we retired to the basement much to the displeasure of Uncle Jim. He enjoyed glancing at Vicki's stunning display of attributes. He tried to be discrete because he was petrified of Aunt Jackie's wrath. But I noticed his stares were starting to linger, so I hastily thanked Aunt Jackie for our Italian delight and suggested that my guest reconvene in the basement.

It was brisk that October evening, so I turned on my gas furnace that resembled a fireplace, and we all started to consume our favorite beverages in cozy, soothing surroundings, a perfect place to spring my diabolical plan. I hated to be such a terrible friend, but since my early sexual abuse, my fixation with women was like a heroin junkie seeking a fix, relentless and laser focused. At half time the Pack was beating the Cowboys by two touchdowns, and Pee Wee was ecstatic. Perfect time to spring my plan into action, but before I could speak Pee Wee started ranting and raving about his favorite topic--aliens, especially alien abductions.

"Shaun, did you know that alien abductions are on the increase. Over 10,000 in the United States alone have claimed to be transported to an alien craft. Many report that the aliens perform medical experiments on them, using a surgical tool to explore their internal organs without cutting them open. The aliens also inserted objects like G.P.S. devices in them, so they could track them once they are released back to Earth," Pee Wee said in an eerie voice sounding a whole lot like Rod Sterling, the weird dude on the old television classic *The Twilight Zone*. I glanced over at Vicki, and her eyes locked onto mine as if to say, "I feel your pain, my boyfriend, and your best friend is highly unstable, so you want to run away with me?" Okay, I embellished the last part of my translation, but it was clear she was tiring of Pee Wee's crazy thought process.

Before I could respond, Vicki chimed in with some sarcasm, "So aliens are tracking human beings just like oceanographers are tracking mammals like whales and dolphins after they place electronic monitoring devices on them? What is the purpose of all the medical and psychological experiments on ordinary everyday people?"

"Well, my dear, don't sound so amazed by their exploratory surgery. Hitler did the same thing during World War II. He wanted to develop weapons of biological warfare, viruses and diseases that would wipe out his enemy. Also wanted to create a super-race that would be under his complete and utter control, the Super S.S. Corp if you will." Pee Wee almost shouted the last part of his reply

The time was right to intervene to save my friend Vicki from an onslaught of nonsense.

"So, Pee Wee, get to the point. What are the aliens conducting all these experiments for?" I asked with a profoundly serious look on my face, like I was a news anchor interviewing a senator or some Hollywood star. An exceptionally long silence followed my question, and then my all-knowing friend spoke, "I believe that when the time is right, knowing the immune system, and all of the other defense mechanisms of the human body, the aliens are going to release a virus so deadly and contagious that it will wipe out all of humanity."

Pee Wee then closed his eyes like some Buddhist monk seeking nirvana.

It was now or never. The drama level had been set. Peewee was obviously drunk, and the Packers were winning by two touchdowns. I voiced my concern about going to my stepfather's home by myself, and I asked if they would like to accompany me on Saturday. I knew that Pee Wee worked every Saturday, so it would be impossible for him to get off since he was in middle management.

"Dude, I got to work, but maybe Vicki can go with you," he said halfheartedly, glancing at his beautiful girlfriend. I faked a look of complete sadness that Pee Wee wouldn't be able to make it. Vicki then completely my wicked plan by stating she was off that day and would be glad to go and be my moral support. I forged a look of deep shock and asked, "Pee Wee, you're going to trust me to spend the entire day with your beautiful, gorgeous girlfriend? He then said the words that will haunt me for the rest of my life, "Shaun, my best friend, I would trust you with my life." That night after they left, I tossed and turned in my bed, feeling like Judas, and I knew that I could not go through with such an evil plan.

CHAPTER 16

The compulsion to be with Vicki was just too powerful. I cursed myself for being so weak, as I rolled out of bed Saturday morning. I tried to call Vicki all day Friday to cancel our plans, but there was a disconnection in my central nervous system. My body would not comply with my mind's desire to do the right thing. I looked at Judge lying on his favorite spot, the bearskin rug right next to my bed. He looked at me with an accusatory stare, and even though it was my guilty conscience, I reprimanded him for being too damn smart for his own good and threatened to withhold his breakfast of left over lasagna, his personal favorite.

I quickly showered, shaved, and got dressed. I packed some kayaking apparel, a colorful swimsuit, a Hilltopper cut off Jersey with the image of Big Red, W.K.U.'s strange-looking mascot on the front. The mascot was a red furry beast with a large gaping mouth that sometimes it would put basketballs or footballs in during games. It was the strangest mascot in all N.C.A.A. sports, but what else would you expect from a university that refers to themselves as the Hilltoppers. I ran up the stairs just as the doorbell rang. As I opened the door, I felt as though I had died and gone to heaven because what stood before me was nothing short of an angel. Her green eyes were shining brighter than a pulsating star, and her blonde hair was in a ponytail that crept down to the small of her back. Her face was perfect even though she wore no makeup, and her smile was radiant and lit up the dark, sad areas in my heart. She had a pair of cutoff overalls on, with a golden bikini top that matched her beautiful, tanned skin, that hinted at a Scandinavian heritage.

I gave her a quick hug, not wanting to give her the slightest hint of the lust that I had for her.

"Sorry, I'm a little early, but better early than late," she said with a slight shrug of her shoulders and a shit-eating grin on her face. I wanted to grab her by the hair like a wild prehistoric caveman and make passionate love to her right there in the foyer.

I swept those emotions away, and calmly said, "Thank you so much for coming with me, Vicki. I haven't seen my stepfather for years. Your presence will deflect some attention off me."

"So, I am just a convenient distraction, huh?" she asked with a fake look of indignation.

"Vicki, your beautiful face would be a distraction for any red-blooded American man," Uncle Jim said from right behind me. I was in such a trance, I didn't notice he and Aunt Jackie sneaking up on us, poised to ask a ton of questions.

"Thank you, Jim, you're so sweet. If you weren't involved with the love of your life, I would dump Pee Wee for you in a heartbeat," Vicki said, winking at my Aunt Jackie.

"Speaking of Pee Wee, where is he?" Uncle Jim asked with one eyebrow cocked up in the suspicious position.

"Pee Wee had to work, and Vicki agreed to accompany me to my stepfather's home at Lake Malone for some kayaking. I will see you all about eight. Don't wait up. I know that's about an hour past your bedtime," I said while whisking Vicki out the front door, hoping to avoid any more questioning that would deepen my feelings of regret and shame.

I walked down to my Jeep and opened the door to my chariot for my angel. I couldn't help but look back at my Uncle Jim who had a look of disappointment on his face because a man of his integrity, values loyalty and honesty above all else.

It was about an hour's drive to Lake Malone. Vicki was quite the outdoorsman, she told me--caribou hunting in Alaska, scuba diving the Caymans, and skydiving over lake Tahoe. She also mentioned she held a fifth-degree black belt in karate. I made a metal note to let her make the first move. I am quite sure she was very attracted to me, or I might be a self-absorbed, narcissistic idiot who was mistaken, in which case I could have my body severely damaged by a woman enraged by the betrayal of my best friend. Suddenly, I realized that Vicki's martial art ability would be the key for me to distract my stepfather while I planted the listening device in his home.

"Vicki, would you mind giving my stepfather a demonstration of your martial arts expertise? He fancies himself a Jackie Chan or Steven Seagal." I said, wanting desperately to explain to her the real reason, but feeling that knowing that my stepfather was an alien would put her life in danger.

Vicky tilted her back and laughed, as if I just asked the most ludicrous question in the world, "Sure, does he have a gym or quarters that we can spar in, and I will give him a hands-on course he will never forget? I will only comply if he asks for such an exhibition. It's the same rule that a vampire has when he cannot come in your home unless invited." After a sexy erection-inspiring wink of her eye, I decided to change the topic of discussion to the person that ironically brought us together, my good friend Pee Wee.

We both agreed that Pee Wee had a huge heart, and we enjoyed his maturity level of about fifteen years old. "He is just so spontaneous and his zest for life is quite contagious. He brightens my world just by being around him, but I think of him more as a good friend than a lover," Vicki confessed.

I was silent during her entire confession, but my dirty mind translated her last statement into "I just wish he had a bigger package" and unfortunately, I laughed out loud.

"What are you laughing about, Shaun? Perhaps a private thought,'" she asked, her voice indicating that she knew exactly what I found to be humorous.

"Oh, nothing, I was just thinking about how I would love to help a damsel in distress," I said rather sheepishly.

I thought she was going to slap me or chastise me for being insensitive, but she grabbed my hand and said, "Who says chivalry is dead?" I knew at that point that Vicky and I were soulmates, but what I didn't know was that many people would die because of our forbidden love.

CHAPTER 17

I was enjoying the conversation with Vicki so much that I was surprised to hear my G.P.S. squawk the familiar "you have arrived." I braked rather hard, leaving skid marks in the road. Thank God no one was behind me on the remote country highway, a shortcut to the most scenic part of the 788-acre lake. Lake Malone served as a reservoir for Logan, Muhlenberg, and Todd Counties in south-central Kentucky. We could barely see the home because of the brilliant red Bradford pear trees that hid it from our view. The random thought popped into mind that my stepfather, the alien, was trying to hide his home from any folks passing by on the road. The house was modest at best for a hot shot fighter pilot and retired senior officer. It was a small home with four small pillars out front and three dog-housed shaped windows on the sloping roof. The front porch had rocking chairs lined up on either side, ready for a big family reunion. A big porch swing built for two, although now empty, was rocking slightly in the warm October breeze. I could see the letters D.M.M. engraved on either side of the front of the house, encased in a white circle. Donna and Mike MacGregor wanted everyone to know who the top dogs in the neighborhood were.

There were many cars parked in the driveway and along the road. I had a sinking feeling that I was going to be surrounded by creatures from another world and began to think of Daniel in the lion's den. I just knew that every alien eye would be on me and Vicki as we entered the house, but to my utter surprise my charming stepdad came out the front door and greeted me with an oxygen depleting bear hug.

"Damn, Shaun, how long has it been? I have missed you," Mike, the Mad Dog, shouted as the top of his voice. He stepped back after almost crushing my rib cage and added, "Whoa, Shaun, she is definitely an improvement over Connie. You're definitely way out of your league." He eyed my date like a ravenous dog eyes a T-bone steak. My stepfather never had much of a filter, and I'm sure at that moment Vicki decided that an invitation to give an exhibition of her martial arts skills would not be needed.

"Listen, Shaun, I want to give you and Vicki a tour of my property," he commented as he led us around to the side of the house. As soon as we turned the corner, both Vicki and I gasped in amazement. A bright red barn stood on the hill, surrounded by emerald- colored grass. The reflection of the barn mixed with the brilliant colors of fall cast themselves on the waters of the small pond that was thirty feet below. The waters of the pond had been treated with Aquiclude, so the mixing of the azure blue and the fall colors was almost magical, a rainbow cast from heaven. Two sandstone layered cliffs surrounded by a retention wall, descended the hill, and seemed to be the source of the eternal flow of water, keeping the pond full no matter the lack of precipitation. I noticed the walkway going down to the dock widened right at the water's edge. Two outside lounge chairs and some rugged metal furniture were placed on a large marble patio, inviting guests to enjoy a day of meditation and relaxation.

"This place has been a labor of love. I created a small dam around my property, but I left a small underground stream flowing into this private swimming hole for the family. The stream feeds the fountain in the middle of the pond, but I can reroute it to the cliffs with a flick of a switch," the stepfather-alien thing said with a hint of divinity.

He was sitting in a hammock that oversaw his kingdom, on a ridgeline overlooking his private swimming hole. He motioned to Vicki and me to sit in the two comfy lounge chairs next to him.

"Notice the walkway around the pond. It meanders over to a little fishing hole filled with channel catfish, crappie, and some brim. Built it with my own two hands, and Donna hand carried all the stones around our little fire pit here. She also designed the little patio at the edge of the pond," Mike said grinning from ear to ear, beaming with pride.

I watched him as he proudly described the construction of his little piece of heaven, hoping to see a twitch in his face or a peculiar reflection of the sun off his eyes, a manifestation of his alien heritage, but there was not even a hint of anything alien about him. He had aged quite a bit. His once brilliant blue eyes were dimmed by years of guilt about how he treated my mother. He had put on some weight, and he had a belly that appeared to have increased in girth, wrinkles had appeared on his forehead, and dark blotches of skin surfaced beneath his eyes. He looked up at me, and smiled showing perfect incisors, like a rabid dog getting ready to strike.

"So glad to see you, Shaun, and thank you for coming. Vicki it is so nice to meet you," he said staring at her for an extended period, breeching all protocol of appropriateness. I was about the reply when he hit the switch that redirected the water from the fountain to the cliffs. A constant stream of water, then flowed down the cliffs, forming two twin waterfalls.

"Tonight, I will turn on the blue and red lights that I have placed inside the cliffs, illuminating the falls so that you will be able to see them for up to three miles away."

I then saw the sign that I had been looking for. When he spoke in his excited tone, his chest never inhaled oxygen at all. His lungs were being filled with a gaseous mixture that was produced within his body. I knew then that my life had always been a lie--a myth-- and I was a lost creature raised by something not of this world.

Chapter 18

M ad Dog Mike MacGregor rose out of his hammock, like a vampire rising out of a coffin, grabbed my date's hand, and started walking up the hill toward his house.

"Come on, Shaun. Want to show you and Vicki the rest of the house before we all go kayaking," he said, walking the women of my dreams up the hill like he had known her for years. I caught the look on Vickie's face. It was one of pure shock, surprise, and disgust, but there was a glimpse of something else, something I would never expect. It was a look of sheer fulfillment. I wanted to rush up to Mad Dog and bash the arrogant bastard in the face, but then I realized that no act or behavior could match my betrayal of my best friend.

Donna met us at the front door and glanced at her husband holding my date's hand and seemed not to care. I suddenly thought that we must be at a swingers' party. Donna was extremely beautiful, with high cheekbones, large deer-like brown eyes that were calm and gentle, and a little pouty mouth. I had the random thought of the fish- like face women make when posing on a dating site. She had long, wavy red hair, tied in a ponytail that flowed down to the middle of her back. She had creamy ivory-colored skin, and high cheekbones.

"Finally get to meet the legendary Shaun MacGregor. Your father speaks of you very highly--great person, kind and intelligent," she said, giving me a long hug. I thought that we might be swapping partners before the end of the night, so maybe I would be able to get the listening device into the bedroom. That would be the perfect place. Everyone knows that pillow talk and intimacy between husband and wife was the best kind of intelligence.

My fantasy was ruined when she turned and looked at her husband. It was a look of complete and utter love and commitment. Vicki finally broke the vice like grip of my stepfather's hand and came over to me, locking her hand in mine. I have never expected the electric current that passed through every atom, molecule, and cell of my body when her hand touched mine. I tried to introduce her to Donna but was too distracted by the pulsating current that ran from the tip of my feet to the hippocampus region.

Vicki grabbed Donna's hand and shook it gently, "Hi, I'm Vicki. It's very nice to meet you.'"

"Charmed, I'm sure," Donna replied cornily with a confused look on her face.

"Now we're like a big ole happy family. Let me give you a guided tour of the rest of our humble home." Mad Dog barked out orders like he was still in the military. We walked into an extremely comfortable-looking living room with two lounge chairs strategically positioned in front of a 48-inch-wide screen television. A leather couch and an old-fashioned rug with ring patterns were laid in the middle of the mahogany floors. An old grandfather clock and a ceiling fan that slowly circulated the gloomy air complemented the furnishings. There were several guests in the room that stared at me as though I were a virus or bacteria under a microscope, and I suddenly knew that I was amid an enemy that wanted to rip my heart out of my chest and eat it.

"Gentleman and ladies, this is my handsome son, with whom I am very pleased," Mike bellowed out like he was an announcer for Monday night football. To my great surprise the entire room broke out into applause with Vicki and Donna clapping the loudest. Suddenly, I had the random, weird thought that they were an alien cult and might be sacrificing me tonight. There was no other explanation for my stepfather's introduction. He had seemed almost sacrilegious because what he said sounded a lot like God's powerful voice resounding in the heavens after Jesus was baptized by John the Baptist in the river Jordan.

"Thank you all for being so kind, but I don't deserve to be held in such high esteem." As I spoke, I briefly scanned the room looking for the weird pattern of breathing that my stepfather had exhibited while on the hammock. With this quick observation, I noticed that a couple of large men sitting on the couch demonstrated the same exhaling without any signs of drawing oxygen into their lungs. My hypothesis was that there were alien duplicates. Using the scientific method, I had converted my supposition to fact.

Mike noticed the red flush on my face. Thinking I was embarrassed by the attention, he ushered us all into his man cave. My stepfather was enormously proud of his spot in the house--wood carvings of every species of duck from Mallard to Mandarin sat on a wooden mantle above the fireplace. Above the carvings was a painting depicting a goldeneye duck in flight.

"So, you're a big duck hunter now, Mike?" I asked trying to get to the bottom of his alien obsession with ducks. Perhaps they worshipped the aquatic bird on his planet.

"Nah, Donna just has a fixation with waterfowl, and you do understand after so many marriages, when Mama's not happy, nobody's happy," he laughed, possibly delighted with himself by making the whole room aware of my dismal record in the department of holy matrimony.

"Take a look at my collection of hatchets. The top belonged to Francis Marion, the Swamp Fox, whose rag-tag militia outwitted the Royal English Marines many times in the backwoods and swamps of South Carolina. The last hatchet on the wall belonged to the Legendary Jim Bowie, who is also known for the Bowie knife. He killed many Mexicans at the Alamo."

Mad Dog seemed to really believe that the hatchets really belonged to these historical figures. I looked at Vicki and she dramatically rolled her eyes, and her smile told me that my stepfather was a goofy, old blowhard.

"The highlight of my mancave, are these tobacco sticks that are shaped like the geographical boundaries of Kentucky." He beamed like he was describing a painting by Picasso.

"Hey, it's almost three p.m., Honey. "Don't you think you should get your son and his beautiful girlfriend on the lake?" Donna interrupted, knowing she was saving us from the ramblings of a narcissistic personality who was obviously a legend, at least, in this own mind.

We made a quick exit to the garage where a sleek fishing boat sparkled in the sunlight.

"This baby has a 300-horsepower, four-stroke engine that can outrun anything on the lake, even those pesky game wardens who are always checking fishing licenses or making sure you're not catching any endangered species like the Loch Ness Monster," Mad Mike said with a chuckle. As I inspected the classic, sleek boat, Mad Mike droned on and on about his prized toy.

"Yea, this boat is equipped with a large live well, fishing rod holders, bait and lure storage, and a casting deck. Speaking of lures, look on the wall. I have them all--Senko worm, crankbait, spinners, and my personal favorites--the Booyah Boo rig, or maybe the bronze eye frog topwater lure. Caught many a largemouth bass with those lures. I could even teach you how to be a champion fisherman with these lures, Shaun," he said, boasting in a loud, obnoxious voice.

Vicki saved the day by pointing to the three kayaks artfully arranged behind the bass boat, "Wow, Orvis Edition Mayfly Jackson Kayaks. Very impressive and very expensive," she exclaimed in a very jubilant shout, unable to contain her obvious relief in not having to be out all day in some substandard inflatable kayak.

"Brought these out yesterday from my storage shed. Nothing but the best for my son and his noble and beautiful lady," he said, eyeing Vicki like a pedophile on crack. I wanted to puke but controlled my emotions.

"Shaun, could you give me a hand loading these on the trailer already hitched up to my truck?" he asked, putting his arm on my shoulders.

I was repulsed by his touch and wanted desperately to shake his alien appendage off me, scared he might pass some ancient, parasitic worm into my flesh.

"Sure," I said, secretly fantasizing that I could knock him to the ground and spearing him with the tip of one of his prized, expensive kayaks. I despised that man or alien or whatever the freak combination.

We drove five winding miles through the backwoods of Logan and Todd County. The holly bushes were a stunning dark green, and the oak trees were dressed up in their finest fall attire. When we finally reached the lake, Mike backed the truck up to the water's edge. I quickly got out of the truck, glad to be free of my alien stepfather. The close confines of the truck made me feel claustrophobic.

Vicki and I both gasped at the beauty that greeted us. The sun was shining, brightly reflecting off the waters with a golden tint, mixed with the rainbow of colors created by the hardwood forest surrounding the lake. Fifty-foot sandstone bluffs rose out from the waters like some monstrous sea creature.

Mike noticed our staring, and said, "Native American Indian tribes like the Blackfoot and Crow used those cliffs as shelter hundreds of years ago, beaching their canoes near the bluffs and building fires underneath the cliffs' protective ledges."

I helped Vicki stabilize her kayak in the aqua-green waters and pushed her off. Then I helped my stepfather into his kayak and pushed him away from the bank. I was the macho, Southern hillbilly making sure the ladies and senior citizens were safe. I sat in my kayak, which was rocking gently in the cool water, and pushed off the shore with my paddle, hoping a didn't capsize five feet from the bank. Mike the alien and Vicki were about 100 yards in front of me making a beeline toward the cliffs. They didn't slow down or wait for me.

"So much for politeness," I thought, as I paddled with an increased urgency, utilizing every ounce of strength that my 6'4" frame could muster. I was acutely aware of my heart issues but couldn't stand the fact that Mad Dog was alone with my future fourth wife.

Suddenly, Vicki stopped paddling and turned her kayak toward me. I had a vision of an angel on earth once again, her hair blowing in the slight breeze, her eyes sparkling like 24-carat diamonds. Her smile was so natural like a wild river in the dazzling sunlight.

"Come on, cardiac boy. Sorry for taking off but being on this beautiful lake was hypnotic and commanded me to paddle like some I was on speed," she laughed, and the radiance of her smile filled me with energy. I was able to paddle up beside her almost immediately. We both laughed, and I touched her hand like we had been dating for years. The attraction and electrical flow between us were so natural it seemed like we had known each other in a past life.

My alien daddy was in the distance, paddling his happy ass off toward the bluffs, his alpha personality mixed with his machismo propelling him toward the cliffs. He was going to be the first to reach them or have a heart attack trying. Then out of nowhere a speeding pontoon boat sent a large wake toward him, capsizing his kayak and throwing him into the cool lake.

I knew there was no time to wait. The lake would cause my stepdad to slip into hypothermia within a few minutes. I reacted as if I were on automatic pilot. I paddled with a strength and stamina that were almost superhuman, thinking that I finally had a chance to show this thing what the hell I was really made of. By saving this creature, I was finally going to get the respect and acceptance I had craved all my life.

When I reached the great Mad Dog MacGregor, he was dog paddling around his kayak, whimpering like a little schoolgirl. The great Mad Dog could not swim. How could a military bigwig not swim? I rolled out of my kayak and grabbed him by the back of his bright orange vest. I started to pull him to the beach under the ledge. I noticed that his lips were already turning a shade of purple. He began to hyperventilate and fight against me, so I pulled him close and slapped the shit out of him, mostly to bring him out of shock, but I cannot deny that slapping him was very satisfying. I finally got him to the bank. He was shivering but still conscious and breathing.

He uttered the words, "Thank you for saving my life," I thought. When I looked in his eyes, I would see a deep appreciation and gratitude, but the look he gave me sent cold chills down my spine. It was a look of shock and surprise because he had underestimated my strength and courage. I knew then he was more than ever determined to end my life because I was a greater threat to his master plan of the complete extermination of human life on earth than he had once thought.

Vicki paddled up with a look of sheer terror on her face. She beached her kayak and to my great surprise kissed my lips with an intensity that almost made me pass out. My body responded to her almost immediately, and I almost had to get in the water to hide my reaction.

After her intense kiss, she stepped back and whispered in my ear, "That was the bravest, most heroic act that I have ever witnessed. You were amazing." Her eyes locked onto mine and I could sense she was sexually aroused. I thought if she gets that turned on about heroic action, watch out little old ladies that need to be escorted across the street or cats caught in trees. Shaun MacGregor will save your ass-- whether you need it or not. We stood there on the beach staring into each other eyes, completely oblivious to my distressed stepfather until we heard him clear his throat,

"Excuse me. Could someone help an old man out? I'm freezing to death," Mad Dog said through clenched teeth.

Vicki went to her kayak and pulled a hoodie out of the storage compartment. She wrapped it around Mike, but now we had a more unsettling problem. We had three people and only one kayak, the others having disappeared far out into or under the water. One of us would have to paddle back and get help; the other two had to stay back and face certain hypothermia because a cold wind was starting to blow out of the north. Being in the best physical shape, Vicki volunteered to go for help, but just as she started to leave, we noticed that the pontoon boat that had caused Mike and me to take an unplanned swim was heading our direction.

The occupants of the pontoon boat included a man in his late forties, his wife, and two teenage sons.

"Sorry about capsizing your kayak," the man said. One of my sons was trying to break the land speed record for pontoon boats. We have tied your kayaks to our boat and want to shuttle you back to the parking area near the restaurant."

We were so happy for the help that Mad Dog kept his mouth shut and accepted the gracious offer. On the way back to our truck, the family wrapped Mike and me in an insulated blanket and gave us all some hot, black coffee from their thermos. By the time we got back to the truck, Mike's lips were no longer blue. He seemed to be his old arrogant self.

We thanked the family for helping us despite the fact they had caused all the trouble to begin with and loaded the kayaks on the truck and headed back to Mike's house and the long-awaited pig roast. On the way back, Vicki almost sat on top of me, holding my hand with an intensity that made me think she had plans to use my body by the end of the night. Mike kept thanking me and praising my heroic deed, and I experienced great inner peace, but if I had known the future, I would have let that alien bastard drown in the depths of Lake Malone.

CHAPTER 19

We arrived at my stepfather's home around 6 p.m. The night had descended on the countryside, and the chirping sound of the crickets intensified with the dark. We could see the blue- and white-colored falls, honoring the University of Kentucky, as we are rounding the curve in the road, about a half-mile from Mike's house. I rolled down the window and could smell the whole 120-pound pig being cooked over an open-fire pit.

"Yea, a true pig pickin is a group effort and an all-day affair. My lovely wife Donna has supervised the entire effort, while I was trying to drown myself in Lake Malone. That pig has been cooked in barbeque sauce for almost five hours now over wood and coals. Hell, two men with shovels must turn the pig about every two hours. How do some pig's feet with beans and slaw sound to you, Vicki?" Mike asked with a hint of a good ole boy accent.

"Sooie pig is all I have to say about that," Vicki said, imitating her best pig call. We all laughed in unison. It was going to be a great night.

We entered the split-level home, and all eyes turned to greet us. Donna came over and gave her husband an intense hug. Mike had called her and explained why we were late.

"Dammit, Mike, I may be a terrible wife, but you don't have to drown yourself to get away from me. Besides, your life insurance policy has to be in effect for a couple years before I can collect on it!" The entire room burst out in laughter.

"Thank God that your loving son was there to save your butt," Donna added, glancing at me with appreciation and love in her eyes. For the second time in one day, the whole room burst out in applause for me. I smiled and accepted the slaps on my back and looks of admiration, but deep in my heart I felt like that pig being cooked outside. They were preparing me for the slaughter.

We quickly showered and joined the festivities. Plenty of beer drinking was part of a good pig pickin. Folks were drinking from a keg that sat on the back porch near the pond and fire pit. The porch was partially enclosed, and a large picnic table sat under the roof. It was ladened with all the fixings like baked beans, green beans, potato salad, fried okra, and all kinds of freshly made desserts. There were also two-person Jacuzzis at each corner of the wooden porch.

I looked around and was surprised to see the porch was unoccupied except for Vicki and me. That puzzled me until I zeroed in on all the folks around the fire pit. They were sitting inside the fumes and smoke. For the first time they all were breathing normal. I could see their mouths opening, inhaling the toxic smoke from the fire, and then I knew the terrible secret--they were all creatures from another world including Mike's beautiful wife Donna.

I retreated from the railing not wanting them to see me, but it was too late, Donna and Mike spotted us and waved, but there was nothing friendly or welcoming about the wave. They waved for us to come down, but I shook my head and pointed to the hot tub. They nodded, but I could feel the cold, dead stares that emitted from their eyes, and it chilled me to the bone. The stare was colder than when I was swimming in the icy Lake Malone. I just wanted to get the hell out of there, but I knew that I had to plant those listening devices before I left.

After dinner, Mike announced that the after-dinner entertainment would involve an exhibition of karate expertise because my beautiful girlfriend was a fifth-degree blackbelt in the ancient martial art. We all gather on the back deck. Mike had set up several stations with several layers of boards to be broken. Vicki would demonstrate her efficiency with both her hands and feet. She appeared to be embarrassed, as my stepfather explained that he was a first-degree blackbelt, but unfortunately, he had gotten injured in his kayaking incident and would not be demonstrating his impressive skills today.

As Vicki approached the first station, every alien eye was on her. Using this diversion, I shrank back in the crowd and proceeded to Mike's study which doubled as a library. I opened the door to the study and examined the ceiling for cameras or other surveillance equipment. Spotting none, I entered the room, preparing to plant the wall phone charger, retrieve Vicki, and get the hell out of this alien crib as fast as possible. I noticed an outlet close to Mike's vast collection of statues of ancient Roman gladiators ranging from Carpophores, who killed twenty animals ranging from lions and tigers to a hippopotamus in one fierce battle, to Commodus, the cowardly emperor featured in the movie *Gladiator* starring Russell Crowe. Commodus sometimes wounded his opponent before a contest, hiding the wound with a breast plate, or making his enemy fight with a wooden sword. I remembered from my Ancient History 312 class at the university that karma finally claimed him when he was assassinated in 192 A.D. Mike also had a large collection of books on ancient astronauts, time travel, and mysterious structures on earth like Stonehenge and the ancient pyramids of Giza, long theorized by scholars to be constructed by aliens as portals to other dimensions.

I placed the phone charger on the back wall, behind the bookshelves, hoping that if Mike spotted it, he would assume that it was his wife's. The device was linked to my cell phone and could pick up conversations from fifty feet away. Just as I plugged the charger into the wall, I heard thunderous applause coming from the back deck. My dream woman must have just completed her demonstration.

I hurried out of the room and joined the group on the patio who was whipped into a frenzy by Vicki's performance. On the deck all around was an abundance of splintered wood on the ground, victims of Vicki's lethal hands or feet.

Someone slapped me on the back and said, "You better watch your mouth with that little lady. She will put you in a body cast." They laughed a sordid alien laugh that angered me a tad, but what really enraged me was the look of unmitigated lust that Mike the alien cast on my precious, deadly, and angelic lady.

We left around ten p.m. amidst protest by the host who wanted us to spend the night, so he could get his alien claws into my lady, I thought. Then I laughed to myself because with Vicki's fighting skills, she would be the aggressor instead of the victim. We forged excuses--I had to work tomorrow, and Vicki had to visit her parents in Russellville.

Mike grabbed my hand and thanked me for coming and saving his life, but his touch felt quite cold and distant, almost alien, I thought, laughing to myself. I hugged Donna, and my favorite alien hugged Vicki for what seemed an eternity.

"Hurry back real soon, Son," Mike shouted from the front door. I thought I would rather spend a long weekend at Western State Mental Hospital in Hopkinsville than come back to this alien hive of Annunaki.

I nodded my head in agreement and yelled back, "See you real soon, Pops," and as I got in the car, Vicki was laughing her head off.

"What the hell are you laughing about?" I asked in a very civil tone, suddenly having more respect for women of the species.

"You know that you would rather me tarred and feathered than to ever visit dear old stepdaddy again," and she winked and smugly giggled, unable to contain her utter delight in my misery.

"Wow, is it the obvious?" I asked. We both started laughing as if we were raving lunatics as I drove away, glancing back at the blue and white waterfall for the very last time--or so I thought. About a mile down the road, Vicki asked me to pull off the road into the parking lot of an old country store that sold everything from fish bait--worms and crickets--to ham and cheese sandwiches. As I turned off the ignition, she leaned over and kissed me, a long, lingering, hot, passionate kiss that took my breath away. I grabbed her, aroused to the full expression of lust, and I knew at that moment, this was the woman I had been searching all my life for.

She suddenly turned away and simply said, "We can't until I confessed to Pee Wee my wicked attraction to you." Little did we know that confession would not happen because our beloved Pee Wee would be dead in forty-eight hours.

Chapter 20

I was rudely awakened by Uncle Jim's harsh Marine yelp permeating the walls of my subterranean lair early the next morning.

"Hey, Benedict Arnold," he shouted at the top of his lungs, mentioning the worst traitor in American history. "You have some guests at the front door."

I could tell by the edge in his voice that he was stressed, so I quickly threw on a Hilltopper jersey and sweats and hurried up the stairs. When I got to the front door, I was greeted by two mean-looking dudes in business suits.

They looked like ex-military, government secret ops types. The biggest muscle bound one said, "Mike wants to meet with you at his lake house, our orders are to pick you, and deliver you to him." He said reaching inside his suit jacket. I said, "Mike who?" and the thug removed his glasses and glared at me with a menacing stare. Just then his cell phone rang, and he didn't even offer a hello. He just handed the phone to me.

"Shaun, this is dear old daddy. I suggest that you get in the car with those kind gentlemen. We don't want to stress out your uncle and aunt. They appear to be rather fragile to me," Mike said in a soft, gentle tone. I turned around to Uncle Jim and Aunt Jackie. Their eyes were wide with alarm.

"Hey, Aunt Jackie, Uncle Jim, my dear old daddy wants to meet with me. Probably forgot something," I said, trying to de-escalate their tension and stress.

As we walked to the sleek, black Suburban, probably armored, and equipped with a sophisticated weaponry system, I waved back at my uncle and aunt and exclaimed,

"Don't wait up folks. Daddy just wants me to forgive him for the bullshit that he put me through all my life."

As soon as the words left my mouth, the trailing goon took my arm and tried to corral me into the S.U.V. I shook his hand off me and told him to get his grubby alien paws off me.

They deposited me in the back seat and closed the privacy curtain. I was left to my wild thoughts and my imagination. Was my dear old daddy going to clone me or place an implant into my brain? Was he going to turn me into some kind Annunaki zombie, controlling my thoughts and making me commit deeds against humanity?

Finally, the Suburban came to a stop, and one of the C.I.A. goons opened the door. I stood in front of a monstrosity, an 8,000 square feet building made of cedar with three giant bay windows that faced Lake Malone and a giant Virginia stone chimney emerging from a sloping roof. It was built against a large sandstone bluff. Nearby were two turrets placed strategically on either side of the house. Close to each was a jacuzzi, both close to the front door. As the goons assumed their positions in front and behind me, I walked up a steep hill, toward the open arms of my alien stepfather who was standing at the front door with a shit-eating grin on his face.

"Wow, Shaun, we go about ten years without contact, and then we have to look at each other two days in a row. You didn't think that little shack three miles down the road was my main home, did you?" Mike asked with that same shit-eating grin on his face. I wanted to slap that grin off his alien mug.

"What the hell is this all about, Mike? Your goons scared the hell out of my aunt and uncle," I said barely able to conceal my anger.

"Not my fault, Shaun. You're the dumbass that has gotten himself smack dab in the middle of an alien civil war, and if you don't agree to my terms today, your uncle and aunt will have much more to fear!"

I was shocked. Not only did he threaten my beloved uncle and aunt, he also admitted that he was indeed an alien and not of this world. I followed him down the long corridor adorned with famous paintings by Da Vinci, Van Gogh, and Michelangelo. It seemed that these aliens had an appreciation for the fine arts and other aspects of human culture.

We entered a large room filled with Tudor furniture. A combination of Gothic and Renaissance carvings depicting biblical or mythological scenes were along the walls.

"You sure do take an interest in human art and culture for a Annunaki servant," I said in a condescending tone as I checked out the room.

"Why not, Shaun? We seeded this planet with life several hundreds of thousands of years ago. We, the fallen angels from the heavens, impregnated earthly women. We have a vested interest in humanity and have controlled every facet of human development for centuries by having a relationship with humans in positions of power from in the White House in Washington, D.C., to the Politburo in Moscow. We control military-industrial complexes around the globe and economic systems ranging from capitalism to socialism. We come from the planet Nubira. We were worshipped by the ancient Sumerians, who built temples and statues honoring us," he replied in a smug, superior tone.

"You mean you have controlled humans through manipulations, cloning, and thought control by inserting implants in humans that have been abducted. The Annunaki manipulate the media, use diverse spiritual dogma, and covert human rights abuse for one purpose--to keep humans in slavery. Using our natural resources like our gold and silver as an energy source to power your crafts and run the major, centralized cities on Nubira. You view us as vastly inferior beings like cattle in the field, and your warlike culture would have terminated the human species thousands of years ago, if we were not helpful as human slaves," I said in a volatile tone filled with hatred and disgust.

"Ah, Shaun, your Indian handler has filled you with hatred. We will be dealing with that Arcturian sympathizer soon. He laughed and a deep guttural sound erupted from his throat."

I was enraged because he had threatened not only my family, but now John Running Bull. I pounced and was within ten feet of his jugular, when a violent invisible force lifted me off my feet and deposited me into a chair that had appeared seemingly out of nowhere. As soon my ass hit the fine fabric, metal clasps closed around my hands and feet.

"Calm down, Shaun! Care for a drink? Being a falling-down drunk, bet you could use one, but unfortunately your hands are preoccupied," he said trying to suppress his laughter.

"Shaun, you're going to sit there and keep your mouth shut because I have a proposition that you can't refuse! Thousands of years ago, we seeded earth with a hybrid species called Nephilim. they became the human elite, men and women that would make contributions to enhance human existence by causing them to evolve into the intelligent, technologically superior people they are today. You may recognize names like Louis Pasteur, Benjamin Franklin, Thomas Edison, Mother Teresa, and George Patton. All these humans and more were Nephilim. Could you imagine how repressed and backward humans would be without these hybrids implanted in this world? Shaun, humans owe us all their worldly possessions, including their own genetic code. We are your creators!"

I shouted out, "You're a damn lying Annunaki bastard!" and as soon as I said those words, one of them covered my mouth with a piece of cloth. I guess They were all serious about keeping my mouth shut.

"Our brethren, the reptilians wanted to devour ancient humans. They viewed the human species as inferior, nothing more than meat sticks to be consumed. We again intervened, compromising to save this planet. We allow the reptilians to be our planetary management team, our regulatory agent managing the natural and human resources with great responsibility and respect. After all, some humans are our half-children. The reptilians are shapeshifters and can assume human form for short periods of time. Shaun, I hate to break it to you, but both most of the world's leaders are shape-shifting reptilians, including members of America's formal governing bodies, the House and Senate.

"Everything was in complete harmony until you started helping those left-wing radicals, the Arcturians, otherwise known as the Watchers. They overlooked flawed humanity--always making excuses for drug abuse, alcoholism, and sexual immorality. They are the great enablers of the galaxy. They view themselves as healers, showing humans technology involving physical healing and incorporating their beliefs and feelings to resolve conflict. They are weak snowflakes and must be exterminated. They are trying to raise human consciousness to a point where it is making it exceedingly difficult for our reptilian brothers to manage life on earth. When you help them with your interventions, you are affecting human destiny, consequently interfering with the plans that we and the reptilians have for our slaves--the human species."

He then peeled the cloth off my mouth.

"The reptilians wanted to terminate your life immediately, and I agreed, that is until you saved my life yesterday during our kayaking excursion. I raised you, Shaun, and have a certain level of compassion and empathy toward you, so I want to offer you a deal.

"Show us your intervention location, and stop assisting these pathetic creatures, and then I will see to your survival," he concluded by releasing the cuffs around my hands and feet as an expression of his supposed deep empathy.

I looked at him like he had at once shed his human form and revealed this true physical form.

"Listen, you alien freak, I will never assist the Annunaki or the reptilians murder this noble Arcturian species who have shown extreme mercy on humans," I said balling up my extremely large fist. He looked at me, and the mask of compassion was gone. I could almost see his alien features twisted up in an expression of rage and hatred.

"Shaun, I will give you forty-eight hours to accept my proposition, and if you decline my offer, you and all the people you love will cease to exist. I just wish those two reptilian assassins would have completed their mission in Turkey. Shaun, you are a Nephilim. I knew what you were the moment I saw you when you were small. I ignored that fact because I loved your mother so much, and I thought I could change your Arcturian D.N.A. through discipline and tough love, but you started demonstrating rebellion, so I ordered two reptilian assassins to murder you. I knew you and your friend Speedy would be at the aqueducts that day, willfully disobeying my commands not to go there. I commanded the reptilian idiots to make the hit look like a couple of pedophiles on a rampage murdered you. Two things I didn't count on was your friend's quick escape and the reptilians wasting valuable time and enjoying pedophilia so much."

"I knew that you were behind my molestation my entire life, but why didn't you ever try to destroy me again?" I asked in bewilderment.

He looked at me for what seemed an eternity and simply replied, "The inner circle of reptilian leaders thought another attempt would bring too much attention to them. Besides we watched as your life spiraled out of control and felt that you were no longer a threat, but that damn Indian helped you discover your gift!"

I felt that a blindfold had been removed from my eyes. I sat there too stunned to speak. I finally looked up and asked, "You mentioned that I was a Nephilim of Arcturian descent. What the hell are you talking about?"

"You have no earthly father, Shaun, your mother was abducted by the Arcturians, and they planted an alien seed in your mother's womb. Talk about misguided loyalties! Shaun, you are assisting the creatures that raped your mother!"

As he told me this horrible truth, a wicked grin spread over his face like the sun spreading light on the earth when it rises after a cold, dark night.

CHAPTER 21

I was still traumatized when the two alien goons dropped me off at my Aunt Jackie's house. I had been given an extension on my life and the life of the people I loved. I had no time to lose. I jumped into my Lexus and drove straight to John Running Bull's home. I drove like a Nephilim madman, running through stop lights, hoping that I wouldn't get stopped by a cop.

I pulled into John's driveway, slammed the door of my car shut, and rocked the whole vehicle with the force of my intense anger and frustration. I was a heat-seeking missile. I didn't notice the grey suburban parked in the driveway.

I banged on John's door, and he opened it with a look of profound peace and understanding and said, "Guess you have spoken to your alien stepfather. Shaun, the anger that you feel is natural, but all of this is a ploy by the Annunaki to attempt to manipulate you."

"Well, I have decided to give them what they want. I need to protect you, my family, and Vicki even after these alien bastards said that they raped my mother.

I then heard John's guest speaking from the living room.

"Now hold on, Hoss. Think you're hitching your wagon to the wrong horses. You have to listen to this old tired cowboy's story before you run off all Helter Skelter." He sounded like an old gunfighter from the wild West, a cross between Wild Bill Hickok and John Wayne.

"Shaun, I want you to meet Bart Mason. He has worked over thirty years for a covert government agency that monitors U.F.O. sightings, alien abductions, implants, and hybrid seeding in the human species," Running Bull said as he led me into his small, quant living room. As I rounded the corner, a huge man standing about 6'5" and weighing about 300 pounds, grabbed my hand and shook it with such vigor that I thought he was going to dislocate my shoulder. He was dead ringer for the ruff and gruff gunslinger lawman Jeff Bridges had portrayed in the movie *R.I.P.D.* He stood there with a wide grin on his face, blue eyes sparking like sapphires, and a large black Stetson hat on his bulging head. It was strange. I liked and trusted this man almost instantly.

"First off, the Arcturians did not rape your mother. They sensed that the Annunaki and reptilians were going to increase their attack on humans, both spiritually and intellectually. The Arcturians chose your mother and seeded her with their D.N.A. without any sexual contact. They needed a soul searcher in the Arcturian bloodline to act as a liaison or ambassador to earth to help end the increased threat of the Annunaki," Bart said as he looked at me with his stern but compassionate stare.

"Hmmm, so my mother was like the Virgin Mary, and I'm some kind of alien Jesus sent down to save all humanity?" I asked sarcastically. Obviously, Bart didn't grasp my smart-ass attitude.

"Damn, John, this boy is smarter than a riverboat gambler!" Bart's laughter was like thunder crashing down from the heavens. I decided to play along, so I asked the obvious question.

"So why after several thousand years of using earth's resources--both human and natural--are the Annunaki increasing their attack on humanity?" I asked.

I will never forget the look of sorrow and despair in his eyes, as he replied with a great gasp of air, "Very simple, Shaun, Nubira, the Annunaki home planet is dying, and its sun will be a supernova soon, destroying every planet in the system. They want to inhabit the planet Earth, but first they must turn it into an environment conducive to their biological makeup."

"So, what type of environment do the Annunaki need to survive?" I asked when I suddenly remembered the toxic air the aliens were breathing around the campfire.

He answered, "An extremely toxic one, full of carbon dioxide emissions caused by hydraulic fracking, and tons of plastic released into oceans and rivers. The Annunaki have instructed the reptilian leaders to abolish any laws that protect the environment. For example, President Tweet removed the United States from the Paris Climate Accord and tied the hands of the Environmental Protection Agency by getting rid of cornerstone laws like the Clean Air and Water Act. The release of methane gas into the atmosphere by hydraulic fracturing will enhance global warming. The melting of the glaciers in both the Arctic and Antarctic Circles that reflect ultraviolet rays from the sun back into the atmosphere will enhance global warming ten-fold," Bart's voice seemed to darken as he spoke.

"The interconnection of life, Shaun, the flooding of many islands and coastal communities will create human suffering of epic proportions as refugees seek asylum in other countries. The problem of Mexicans crossing the borders in the southwestern states will be trivial compared to the sheer number of worldwide immigrants seeking refuge if those ice caps melt. There will weeping and gnashing of teeth, wars, famine, and genocide as the humans are displaced like never before." John Running Bull uttered these words. My mind began to realize the enormous amount of horror the Annunaki were going to force on us.

I knew that the Annunaki was going to create misery on the human species, misery of epic proportions, but I could not put my family in jeopardy. I calmly told them both that I was going to help the Annunaki and was heading toward the door when Bart's voice barked out a solution to this incredible quagmire.

"We will protect your entire family, Shaun," he bellowed at the top of his lungs.

"How?" I asked. "You have a witness protection program to protect my family from the Annunaki?" I asked him, my eyebrows raised in a comical fashion.

"As a matter fact, we do, Shaun. When you were a kid, did you ever watch *Star Trek*?" he asked.

"What are you going to do? Transport my entire family to another time and place?" I asked with a smirk on my face.

"Damn, ole Hoss! You're as sharp as a tack. That's exactly what we're going to do, except we would bring your family back when the Annunaki threat is non-existent or we kill all those sons of bitches!" He laughed, and the walls vibrated with elation.

I stopped and turned around, and with wide eyes asked him.

"How?"

"Well, Shaun, there are places on earth that are teleporters into different dimensions--Stonehenge in Great Britain, the Easter Islands off Chile. We have known for years that both these places have transported aliens from one dimension to another.

"Well, Hoss, how am I going to get my entire family to Great Britain or Chile?" I asked in a mimicking good ole boy tone.

"Aw, Shaun, I'm one foot ahead of you. There are many natural places that can be used as transport areas with the help of our friends the Arcturians. These places have paper-thins walls between dimensions. There are many such places worldwide, but according to my research the two closest to you are the Natural Bridge in the Red River Gorge and Seventy Six Falls, both in Kentucky." He then winked at me, and I knew that he relished the fact that he was one step ahead of me.

I stood there frozen with my indecisiveness, and finally said that I would tell them of my decision in the morning. Now I only had forty hours before my stepfather would unleash the reptilian hellhounds to terminate my life and the lives of those that I cared the most about.

"So, we can all just get beamed up like they told Scottie to do on *Star Trek*?" I asked sarcastically.

"Sure, we can, Shaun. Listen! We have given you a lot to think about tonight, so call us in the morning to let us know your decision but remember the fate of humanity lies in your noble hands."

"Nothing like a ton of pressure on your heart and mind to help you sleep like a newborn baby," I whispered as I headed for the door.

"Oh, Shaun, before you leave, I want to give you a weapon to defend yourself against the Annunaki or their reptilian brothers. Bart then handed me some syringes filled with nothing. I looked at him with an inquisitive look on my face and asked.

"What the hell am I supposed to do with these empty syringes?"

"These syringes are filled with pure oxygen. Inserted into the heart of reptilians, the syringes will kill them faster than Raid will kill cockroaches. I know these damn syringes will work. Killed a few aliens in my time." He said rather sternly, and then a look or profound hatred spread over his face. I knew that I was dealing with a bad-ass hombre, and I asked, "Are you C.I.A., F.B.I, or just a Man in Black affiliated with a covert operation, assassinating aliens that threaten humans?"

"Son, I am all those plus a couple more, and If I tell you the truth, then I will have to kill ya!" as he said this old cliché, he threw his shaggy head back and laughed, and it sounded eerily familiar to a wolf baying at a full moon. I then realized the ghosts of my past were going to pay homage to me in the most gruesome manner.

CHAPTER 22

I left bewildered and in a state of shock. It didn't help that before I left his house, John Running Bull grabbed my hand and like a real father said, "Son, I know you will do the right thing!"

The last thing I ever wanted to do was disappoint my mentor and friend. It was around 5:30 in the evening, but I didn't want to go home because my Uncle Jim could sense tension and stress like a Republican could sense a bleeding-heart liberal. For some insane reason working has a calming effect on me, so I turned on my ride-sharing app and headed toward Nashville International Airport. It would be a decision that I would regret for the rest of my turbulent life. That one decision would alter the course of destiny for not only my family but also for my Arcturian brothers.

I navigated to the area designated for ridesharing and for-hire vehicles. Old Charlie, the gatekeeper, greeted me with a grin and a wave, his bald head and diminutive stature almost comical. He craved power after serving almost thirty years on the Metro Nashville police force. His uniform was immaculate, cleaned and pressed to perfection. He marched out of the guard shack, walking with a slight limp and asked for my identification.

"Damn, Charlie, you know me. Why do I have to show you anything?" my voice had a little edge, curiosity of my horrifying day.

"Ah, big brother is watching me now," he replied in a gruff masculine voice, as he pointed to the cameras on the roof of the guard house.

"Seems like some damn kids on the night-shift are allowing their friends to loiter. Damn hard to find good help these days. What the hell are you doing here so early, Shaun? You usually are here late at night, trying to get a hot flight attendant on a layover," he said chuckling.

"Yea, Charlie, you know me. Always on the prowl, or at least until I met the love of my life," I laughed thinking of the night with Vicki, my new heartthrob.

"Do tell, my friend. Old men need to hear of a young man's adventures. Helps us to remember that we had a set of balls at one time." He laughed with gusto, his bald head glistening in the light of the guard house.

I was about to tell him of my new love when my app started pinging, instructing me to pick up Jill at the lower concourse.

"Seems as if I have a damsel in distress at this very moment. I will tell you all about it my friend after I service Jill."

I backed the car up and waved at my good buddy, never anticipating that it would be the last time I would ever see him.

Jill was sitting on the bench reading a cosmopolitan magazine when I pulled up. At first, I thought she was a fashion designer. Her blonde hair was in a tight bun, and her exposed neck and ears were encased with ultra-expensive jewelry. The diamonds were so large on her earlobes that they had to be fake. I mean what kind of moron would make themselves a target for violent crime. I estimated that they were at least 3,000 dollars a set because my ex-wife Carla was a gold digger and wanted some earrings exactly like what Queen Jill was modeling, so I sent Jill packing.

She stood up and had to be about 6'5", an Amazon woman. She had extremely dark eyes that radiated a coldness and detachment that chilled me to my core, and for a moment I had an urge to cancel the trip and get the hell away from this voodoo princess. I got out, and opened the back door for her, ushering her in the backseat with a wave of my hand, proudly welcoming her to the Burger King car where she would have everything her way. She wrinkled up her nose and looked at me like I was a piece of dog crap on her expensive designer boots. I quickly returned to the front seat, and she immediately requested that the privacy window be activated. I complied, internally debating whether to give her a shot of tranquilizer because the Arcturians were not sending me a strong signal. In other words, the bars on my reception were extremely low. I now wonder if I just wanted to give her an intervention because I just didn't like the bitch.

After I had confirmed that I picked Jill up, the app gave me the drop off location, Lebanon, Tennessee, a community outside Nashville, about 30 minutes away.

Jill rolled down the privacy current. "Sir, do you have any refreshments, like bottled water or a snack? I am simply starving after my long flight," she whined in a surprising low voice. I silently wondered if she was a man in drag, the sheer size of this queen and her low voice scared me.

"No, ma'am, you're my first ride, and I simply haven't had time to pick up snacks yet, but you're in luck I have some watermelon gum here," I said silently hoping that she was not going to give me a one-star rating.

Her response clinched it for me. "Do I look like a cheap whore to you? No, I don't want any damn gum. You're very poorly prepared, which will reflect on the rating you're getting. Just stop at a damn McDonalds. Think you can handle that?" She said the last part in a condescending tone.

"Well, bitch, you aren't getting a happy meal. You're getting two doses of phenobarbital and diazepam," I thought, as I pushed the button to raise the privacy curtain. Once it was up, I hit the lever to release the dogs of war into her beefy-ass neck. As I neared the intervention point, I could hear the beast snoring in the back seat. I parked in the old barn and set up the pulsating lights. That's when the shit hit the fan. I opened the door to the back seat and put my fingers on her carotid artery. The vision that I saw would haunt me forever.

It was Nashville, but a toxic cloud of radioactivity hung over the city like a blanket. The Cumberland River was awash with pollutants, like raw sewage, plastics, and carcinogenic runoff from chemicals like benzene and cross alphas used in the hydraulic fracturing operations downriver. The river was so clogged that it resembled a filthy lake. Stench rose from the stagnant water and made my nasal passages burn. People in my line of sight looked like firefighters waging war against a chemical fire or doctors combatting a deadly virus. They had full-face respirators and personal protective gear on from head to toe. It was obvious that this toxic environment was completely hazardous to humans.

I was so fixed by my vision on my passenger. I didn't feel this thing move, but I heard its reptilian voice clearly as it used the human voice box to translate its message of complete hatred for the human species.

"Ah, Shaun, how do you like your planet Earth in the future. My species and the Annunaki will thrive for centuries in this new environment while the human species will become extinct. It's just too bad that you will not be around to witness your species' demise." It then pounced on me, its artificial human flesh hanging off its reptilian scales like rotting wallpaper. It wrapped its claws around my neck. It was on top of me, its glowing yellow eyes inches from my face. Its breath smelled like a rancid sewer. As the human camouflage began to peel off. I could make out a large tail wagging back on forth, like it was a dog happy to see its master. My airway was completely sealed off, and my consciousness was fading. I just couldn't believe that I, Shaun MacGregor, the last soul searcher on earth, would perish this way.

I then remember the oxygen syringe in my front pocket. Somehow, I moved my hand down and felt the syringe. I clenched my hand around it, and with superhuman or Arcturian strength managed to shift my weight enough to throw my reptilian assassin off balance. I brought the syringe up with lighting quickness and plunged it deep into the thoracic cavity of the beast. It screamed and began to hyperventilate or whatever its opposite non-oxygen breathing equivalent was, clawing at its own throat. It gasped for air, like a fish out of water, or a human submerged in water. After what seemed an eternity, it opened the car door and walked about two feet collapsing in the tall grass near the barn. As soon as the damn thing got out of my car, I climbed in the front seat and gunned the engines. When I had driven a few miles, and the flight or fight response had dissipated from my body, two thoughts invaded my subconscious. My dear old stepdaddy violated his 48-hour guarantee or that my Arcturian brothers had conspired to assassinate me, fearing that I had become a Annunaki double agent.

CHAPTER 23

I was in panic mode and drove my Lexus like a madman down I-65, passing cars with wild abandon. It was around 5:30, but the night had already descended upon the countryside. I weaved in out of cars, like one of the hoods caught on a video demonstrating the wildest police chases. To my amazement, I made it to the exit for Highway 25, the rural country road that would lead me to Aunt Jackie's, where I would find my family safe and sound. In retrospect, that was a very unrealistic expectation.

When I reached my Aunt Jackie's, the front door of their ranch style home was wide open. At that point I knew the carnage that I would discover upon searching the home. My heart was in my throat, and my hands were visibly shaking when I reached the house. The first thing to assault my nostrils was the coppery scent of blood. Bile began to build in the back of my throat. Tears welled up in my eyes. I walked into the living room, and blood was caked on the walls. High velocity blood spatter was on the floor, indicating blood spurting from the femoral or carotid artery. I knew that I didn't need to contaminate the crime scene, but I couldn't help myself. My aunt and uncle were the only parents that I have ever had in my pathetic life.

My Uncle Jim was in his chair, obviously beaten to death, before he could even react to the threat in his own home. The bastards didn't even let my eighty-five-year-old uncle out of his chair. I was sure his Marine spirit was restlessly walking the earth looking for the cowards that didn't even allow him dignity in death. He was beaten so badly that both eye sockets were completely ruptured, and both eyes were hanging on his cheeks by a tendon. His skull bone was protruding through his hairline, fractured, and broken. Every inch of his lower torso was covered with contusions and bruises. It was obvious he was tortured before death.

With tears streaming down my face, I got up and found Pee Wee's body alongside my Aunt Jackie's body in the kitchen. The conditions of both bodies were distinctly different from my uncle's. There was not a mark on them. In fact, both appeared to be sleeping on the floor, as if they had consumed something that caused them to lose consciousness rapidly. As I got close to my Aunt Jackie, I noticed a hairline incision encircling my aunt's forehead. I was in shock, so I nudged her head with my foot. The top portion of my beautiful Aunt Jackie's cranium slipped into the floor, and to my complete and utter horror her skull was completely empty. Her brain was gone!

My mind was reeling. I was losing consciousness from shock, but before the blackness closed in on me, I thought, "How weird!" When the top of her head slipped onto the floor, it reminded me of a Jack-O-lantern when you removed the top portion and looked inside to see a candle glowing brightly.

I passed out.

I don't know how long I had been out, but when I woke up, the home phone was ringing off the hook. It was like an alarm clock beckoning me to consciousness. I shook my head, trying to clear the cobwebs. I stood up, glancing down at my friend Pee Wee, and realized that he had the Titan jersey that I had bought for him for Christmas. He loved it because it displayed his old high school football number 13. In his childhood mind, part of him had made it to the pro's. I went over and noticed the same surgical incision was circling his forehead. I assumed his brain was gone too but couldn't bring myself to desecrate another corpse to look. Funny how you think of absurd and comic things, when surrounded by extreme horror. I think it's like a human defense mechanism. Judging from Pee Wee's immature impulses, I wondered if his brain was as small as his Manhood. I then started sobbing thinking of my betrayal of my best friend with his love Vicki.

"Vicki!" I screamed. She is in danger too. I quickly dialed her cell phone and left a frantic message. I told her to call me as soon as possible. I then ran downstairs and knew that if someone had killed Judge, I would just put my 9mm to my head and blow my brains out. In retrospect, if I had known my future that might have been the humanitarian thing to do.

I found Judge in the closet, whimpering with fear. It took me a moment to coax him out of the closet, but when he recognized me, he leapt into my arms. His whole body was trembling with fear. I tried to sooth him with my calming voice, telling him he was now safe, but he kept on shaking like a leaf. I then remembered that Judge had never been afraid of anything. While camping, he had encountered a couple of coyotes around the tent and approached them with such ferocity that both retreated into the woods. Whatever came to the house that night must have surely been the spawn of Satan.

Time was wasting, so I packed some rations for myself and Judge--clothing for me, food for Judge--and exited the basement door. I ran to my Lexus and opened the back door for Judge to jump in. When I was behind the wheel, my chest was exploding with pain, and I got my nitroglycerin pills. I glanced at my cell phone and was upset that Vicky had not yet called back and had not even sent a text.

I quickly dialed 911 and screamed, "There has been a triple homicide at 1523 Old Pike Way, Springfield, Tennessee. No need to send an ambulance. And the crime scene is contaminated."

When the 911 operator asked for my name, I slammed the phone down. An instant later, I realized that my D.N.A. would be all over the crime scene, so now not only the Annunaki but the entire police force of Middle Tennessee would be searching for me.

I downloaded Vicki's Nashville address into my G.P.S. and headed to Nashville. My cell phone began to explode with John Running Bull's ringtone, the theme song to the movie *The Last of The Mohicans.*

"Running Bull, my whole family has been slaughtered by the Annunaki. I am on the run!" I screamed into the phone.

"Shaun, calm down, my son. We have a plan for extraction. Get to Hillbilly Kayak Rental near Adams, Tennessee, as soon as possible. We will be waiting for you," he said with an eerily calm voice, like he had anticipated this whole nightmare.

"What, the fuck? I'm running for my life, not going on vacation!" I hotly yelled into the phone.

"Shaun, this is Bart. I knew that the Annunaki would not honor that 48-hour agreement, so I planned your extraction. I will have you extracted in 72 hours, but you must trust me. This is not my first rodeo!" Bart's low-pitched Southern twang echoed in my ears.

"Well, I'm sorry to delay my extraction, but I have to get Vicki. Her life is in danger," I said with a certain degree of defiance.

"Proud to tell ya, son, that my boys have already picked her up, and she is safe and sound, eagerly waiting for you. Told you this wasn't my first rodeo. Now get your ass here pronto," he barked.

I set my G.P.S. for Hillbilly Kayak. It was 8:30 at night and pitch black. I took another nitro and began to weep with great heaving sobs. Then I heard a voice. It was like a supernatural voice from my dear old alien stepdaddy, "Quit your damn crying, Soul Searcher, because before this is over, we are going to give you something to really cry about." I then thought about navigating the cold waters of the Red River in the middle of the night, and goosebumps began to multiple on my flesh.

PART TWO

The Annunaki

◆

October 19th
The Present Day

CHAPTER 1

B y the time I reached Hillbilly Kayak in Adams, Tennessee, it was around 10:30 p.m. There were log cabins that resemble shacks that would have existed in the hills of Appalachia years ago. I could barely see the front porch, but I envisioned a mountain man sitting there smoking a corncob pipe and drinking 100-proof moonshine. There were five or six cottages in a semi-circle for folks that hated camping. I then noticed several tents down on the sloping hill near the river. Campfires illuminated the tents and reminded me of a Boy Scout jamboree. I relished that childhood memory of pure joy and happiness before my soul was darkened forever.

I got out of the car, and my senses were on high alert as a figure was running at me with an urgency that unnerved me. Then Judge took off like a bullet and jumped up and into the shadow's arms. I then knew that it had to be Vicki, and when she got close, she almost flung her body at me. The force of that reunion almost knocked me down. She hugged me with such an intensity that a spectator to our reunion would think she had not seen me in years.

"Shaun, I have been worried about you. Please tell me that aunt, uncle and Pee Wee are not dead, and this is a bad dream." Vicky wailed.

"I'm sorry, Vicki. They are all dead and our lives are in grave danger. I have been calling you for several hours. Where have you been?" I said with tension and stress in my voice.

"Shaun, I was at my parents' house in Russellville. We were all going to the tobacco festival in the morning. Every year they reenact

Jessie James' bank robbery in 186. I loved that part. A fake gunfight and real horses are very stimulating. I turned my phone off because Mom and I were playing Scrabble and didn't want to be disturbed," she said, her voice filled with pain, partly spawned from her betrayal of my best friend.

I now remembered her telling me her parents lived in Russellville, a small hamlet fifty miles north of Nashville. I recalled from my history studies at W.K.U. that Russellville was indeed a town particularly important to Kentucky history. John Crittenden, who represented Kentucky in both the House and Senate and author of The Crittenden Compromise, lived in Russellville from 1811 to 1818. The compromise, designed to legalized slavery in the Constitution, failed to pass, but Crittenden went on to serve as Attorney General in two administrations.

Vicki absolutely had glowed when she talked about being the captain of the cheerleading squad of the first-ever Panther state championship football team in 1980. She was most proud of the history of Rhea Stadium. The stadium has been renamed Ken Barret Field, for the legendary coach who guided his program to three state championships in 1980, 1983, and 1990. This football town, rich in tradition and starved for a state championship team since the 1930s, awarded the great coach for finally delivering the crown jewel, not once but three times.

Vicki then continued her description of the stadium. The stadium was constructed during the Great Depression under the Works Progress Administration as part of the New Deal. From Ninth Street in the town, the stadium appeared to be a Civil War fort and dared any Friday night rival to scale it and invade Panther territory. The wall, an Art Deco masonry masterpiece, is approximately 12 feet and meanders along Ninth Street for about half a mile. It is listed on the National Register of Historic Places and features the faces of sports legends of the era--Jack Dempsey, Jim Thorpe, Ty Cobb, Paavo Nurmi, and Red Grange.

I remember her telling me of her walk along Summer Street that headed south toward Main Street one glorious Friday night. Her vivid description of the stadium built on a sloping hill with the roaring crowd sitting in the bleachers like Roman citizens cheering for modern-day gladiators. The Press Box marked with "Rhea Stadium" was built into the southern wall. It was centralized and as if were the Roman Coliseum, all the nobility including the emperor would be there. Vicki said she could visualize the man giving a thumbs up or down at the end of the fight.

She then told me that what really gave a full picture was the mammoth homes. Each was two stores with sloped roofs and large concave bay windows across Ninth Street facing the three flag poles. One displayed the U.S. flag, another a Russellville Panther flag, and finally, the last, the commonwealth of Kentucky Flag. She said as she peered up from the street, the lower wall, field, bleachers, upper wall, and finally the monster homes were aligned in geometric perfection. The scene coupled with the lights towering over the field and the beautiful fall colors of the maples and oaks that lined Ninth Street were like a work of art from God, perfect and divine during football season.

I studied her face for a moment, and somehow, she was glowing with inner beauty, heightened by the lumination of the full moon above us.

"Where are the others?" I asked, not quite sure I wanted to know.

"They are in the rental office. Bart and John are anxiously awaiting you. They want to brief you on our extraction. Shaun, Bart, and John told me all about your gift, and how you are in the middle of an alien civil war. This is all bazaar and insane, and I resent your endangering my life as well as your best friend and family. I have a good mind to beat all your butts and drive home."

Her gaze was intense and angry, but I sensed another emotion--one of sheer excitement. Perhaps she was just an adrenaline junkie.

"I am so sorry and ashamed to get everyone involved. Now three of the people that I love the most are dead, but this is bigger than the both of us. The continual survival of humanity depends on what happens in the next forty-eight hours. I am sorry Vicki, but you are now in danger, and I couldn't live with myself if something happens to you. Please believe me. This is real, and you will perish unless you are extracted," I pleaded in a broken, emotional tone.

The silence of the night was pierced by Bart's voice, "Get your butt up here, Hoss. We have a lot to cover before we push off. Hope you're ready for a long-distance kayaking trip."

Vicki and I hugged for a moment, and I held her hand as we walked together toward the rental building. When we reached it, John Running Bull gave me an overwhelming hug, He had tears in his eyes as he explained that he thought I was dead.

Bart was standing in the middle of the shack, flanked by two men that I had never seen before. They were big, burly men, rugged-looking, like a couple of lumberjacks. There were three or four chairs in the room, so John, Vicki, and I sat down and glared at the three colossal men standing in front of us.

"Time is of the essence. We have thirty-six hours to navigate the generally tame Red River through the Red River Gorge. We will travel from six in the evening until six in the morning.

I interrupted with an asinine question.

"Why are we traveling at night, and why are we traveling by river like some wild Indians in the 1800s?" I asked, in a slightly agitated tone.

Bart and the two other men glared at me, and in then his thunderous voice, he roared, "Don't interrupt me again, Shaun. If I don't address your concerns in my briefing, I will answer all your questions at the end. We have done this several times, and I demand your respect and your patience. If you can't follow my instructions, my team will leave you at the mercy of the Annunaki, and believe me, my Hoss, they would have no mercy, as you already have deduced. Look, I realize the day has been traumatic for you, but you must obey my instructions for the next two days. Is that clear?"

I was about to reply with some smart-ass remark when John Running Bull grabbed my leg.

"Sure, Bart, you have my unwavering attention, just been a bad day," I replied slightly bowing my head as a sign of respect.

Bart's voice softened, realizing the horror that I had experienced in the last twelve hours.

He then addressed my concerns, "We have to travel 100 miles by river to the extraction point, the Natural Bridge, located about six miles east of Slade, Kentucky. We will use the river because every policeman in Kentucky is at this very moment is searching for you, Shaun. Your D.N.A. was all over the crime scene. The Annunaki are also are looking for all three of you because they know that you both are assisting the Arcturians, so you are a threat to the master plan that they and the reptiles have for the destiny of humanity. Vicki, my dear, you are just collateral damage.

We are traveling at night because the Annunaki recharge their breathing devices at night. They entered a decompression chamber and the breathing device that gives them the toxic methane and carbon dioxide mixture they breathe during the day is recharged. Each of you will be equipped with night-vision goggles, but there will be a full moon for our entire trek. We will rest at areas that I have selected in advance because they provide the most camouflage and natural cover. Finally, everyone will wear a special kind of lotion during the day but not for sun protection. This lotion will shield you from the infra-red heat-seeking scans on the Annunaki spaceships. That's about all you need to know now. Are there any questions?"

"Yea, Bart, introduce us to your team," Vicki chirped.

"Of course, Vicki, I almost forgot. These men know the Red River currents, rapids, and twists and turns like the back of their hands."

As he turned to the towering red-headed beast to his right, he said, "This is Dick List, but prefers to be called Richard for obvious reasons. You will always want to stress the t in his last name; I would hate to upset our main guide." Bart was trying hard to suppress a major hee-haw.

He turned to the lumbering Black man who had to be at least 6'6". He had dark, longish, curly hair and brooding deep brown eyes. "This is Blackjack. He knows the woods surrounding this area. He will also be responsible for bringing all the supplies we need for the whole trip--sleeping bags, tents, and provisions."

"It's almost 6:30. You have thirty minutes to get yourself mentally prepared for our journey. Shaun, can I have a word with you alone?" It was a command not a question, so I patted Vicki's hand and told her I would meet her outside.

When Bart I was alone, he told me some news that shocked me to my core,

"Shaun, when the police arrived, they only found one body at the house. Your uncle. His entire body was bruised and was broken, his head smashed in. Your prints were all over the house. Forensic folks think that you beat your uncle because of some unmitigated rage."

I was in a state of shock. I had seen my aunt and best friend on the floor, absent their brains. I looked at Bart, my eyes wide with fear as I tried to think of the reason their bodies were missing.

"Bart, that was why Judge was trembling with fear. The Annunaki were still in the house," I speculated.

"Yea, Shaun, that's what I have been thinking, but why didn't they apprehend you then? I can't figure it out," Bart answered, his huge forehead wrinkled in deep concentration.

"Bart, why do you think their brains were missing," I asked in a hollow voice, already knowing the answer.

"Shaun, I think you know that answer to that. These vile, evil bastards are planning to clone your beautiful aunt and your buddy Pee Wee.

CHAPTER 2

I was almost out the door when Vicki announced that she was not going with us.

"Shaun, I just can't accompany you because this is madness. My parents will be devasted if I should just vanish like a phantom in the night," she said with her arms folded across her chest, signifying that her mind was made up.

"For God's sake, Vicki, you and your parents will die if you don't listen to me. The Annunaki have no mercy. Besides, you have been selected by the Arcturians to assist me in saving humanity. This is your destiny!" I was almost begging for her to join us.

"I'm sorry, Shaun," she said as she walked over to hug me. I had no other option. Desperate times call for desperate measures. I grabbed her hand and wrist. I fully expected to get kicked in the mouth, but she just stood there like she was in shock. I was deeply ashamed and hurt. My vision showed a much younger Vicki being raped by a much older man. She was screaming and begging the older, stronger man to stop. He was full of lust and was violently pumping his manhood into her young, virgin vagina. I began to weep and released her hands.

I was sobbing, so she put her arms around me, thinking that I was upset because she wouldn't be coming with me.

"Vicki, I'm so sorry for what happen to you when you were a teenager," I said with tears running down my face. She stepped back, a look of sheer bewilderment and surprise on her face.

"What are you talking about, Shaun?" she asked knowing that I knew about her deep, dark secret.

"Vicki, I know that you were raped. My gift allowed me to peer within your soul, and I wish I could erase that image from my mind."

"Yes, Shaun, I was viscously raped. That's why I earned a fifth-degree black belt. I was never going to allow myself to be that vulnerable ever again." Her eyes were filled with either anger or surprise. Even in the bright moonlight. I could not tell which. I turned to go, shamed by my uninvited glance into her soul.

"Wait, Shaun! That proved to me that you are indeed gifted with second sight, and if all mankind's existence depends on my going down this river in the middle of the night, then who am I to oppose the wish of the universe. But what happens to my parents if I should go with you?"

"I promise you by accepting this mission, the Arcturians will protect your parents even though they don't actively get involved in human affairs. They will find a way to keep your parents safe until you return."

A loud voice pierced the darkness, "Time is wasting. We are burning darkness here. Get your asses down here." Bart's voice was full of anxiety born not of fear for his own safety but for ours.

"I believe we're being paged," I said, and I grabbed Vicki's hand. We ran to the river with our hearts pounding in our chest, ready to fulfill our destiny. Judge followed behind us, happy to be with his master.

As we reached the water's edge, Bart was standing before me blocking my view of the river.

"I'm sorry, Hoss, that dog can't come with us. He would just slow us down."

"Well, Hoss," I echoed, "if the dog doesn't go, then I'm not either," I said, and I guess the intense passion in my eyes convinced Bart of my sincerity.

"John told me that you would not go unless the dog went too, so I purchased this 30-foot tandem kayak with an attached rudder so even with your canine passenger, you should be able to make it through high winds or strong currents." He then stepped aside so I could inspect the mode of transportation that would carry us to the extraction point. It had a glide-track foot brake and thigh pads for a stable response. It was an incredible boat, but Judge and I would still need a miracle to paddle a hundred miles without incident. Could he lie motionless in his roomy compartment for twelve hours a day? I shuddered at the thought.

"I guess he can ride with you in this specialized kayak, but can that mutt swim?" Bart asked, his eyebrows raised in a skeptical position.

"Like a damn dogfish," I replied, a faint smile on my lips. "Judge is very intensely bright and well disciplined." So, I led him to the boat, positioning him in the back compartment near one of the thigh pads.

"Now, Judge, lie down, heel, and be still, boy," I commanded him with the sternest look I could muster. He looked at me and cocked his head to one side as if to say, "Just get in the damn boat, Shaun. I got this."

"Okay," Bart noted, "but if he slows us down, you will have to leave him behind at one of our camping sites. Everyone will be carrying their tent and sleeping bags in the front of the kayak. Just think of it as an incentive not to capsize. If you go into the river, it is going to be a long, cold, wet day for you until the sun comes up," Bart said with a slight grin on his face.

Dick and John were already in the river, their kayaks sitting in shallow water, not impacted by the gentle current of the Red River. Blackjack was in a large canoe, which was laden with supplies, food, and camping gear.

I pushed Vicki off the bank. Then I used my paddle to push myself off the shore. Out of the corner of my eye, I saw Blackjack push the canoe out into the water. We formed a box around Blackjack's canoe. His canoe would stay in the middle, his precious cargo protected from any unseen debris or wood floating in the river. Since he knew this river better than anyone, each of us was within hearing range of his voice when he gave us instructions.

"This is the squad wedge formation used in the army. Keep your lights off unless we tell you to illuminate them. We will have rally points every two hours to check the status of each boat and operator. Let's go!" Bart shouted as he took the lead position on the left side of the river. John Running Bull's kayak was positioned forty feet from his on the right side. The rear formation had me in the middle, Vicki forty meters to my right, and John List forty meters to the left.

The moon shone down upon us and illuminated the shore. The maples and oaks, dressed up in their fall colors, acted as boundaries on either side of the river and beckoned us forward. During the first five miles, I was amazed by the shining eyes of the foxes, coyotes, or other nocturnal wildlife as they watched us paddle down the river, wondering why we were invading their habitat in the middle of the night.

I looked over at Vicki, paddling with grace and agility, her stamina and strength amazing to behold. She sensed me looking at me and smiled. She was completely at peace here on the river.

After two hours of steading paddling, Bart stopped and waited for the rear guard to catch up. As soon as Vicki and I arrived, Bart asked if everyone was okay. Blackjack explained that we would be traveling close to the Bell Witch Cave entrance. He then proceeded to tell the story of the supernatural, clairvoyant witch that haunted the farm of John Bell from 1817 to 1821.

"The Bell Witch occupies the cave that opens along the Red River. Explorers think that the cave meanders for about 15 miles. Legend says that the Bell Witch can cross long distances with superhuman speed. I am telling you this because the current in the river gets weird in this area. It's kind of like the Bermuda Triangle of the Red River. I have seen many kayakers get in deep trouble in this area. The current forces everyone into a narrow channel filled with submerged branches and undergrowth. So, beware, and if you feel like you're caught in an undertow, just relax. Don't fight it. Save your energy to get your water-filled kayak to shore." Blackjack's eyes shined with horror as he explained this supernatural legend that has been around for over two hundred years.

I almost laughed at the absurdity of his story and dismissed it as folklore. We paddled on for about half a mile when the cave's opening suddenly appeared on my right. Vicki and I passed the cave with no spooky undercurrents affecting our craft, but Dick List was not as fortunate. His kayak looked like it was caught inside an underwater tornado. I quickly turned on my headlight and yelled for Bart and John to stop. Judge started barking with a sudden ferocity as if he was asking, "Why were we not helping our stricken companion. I tried to paddle toward the incapacitated kayak, but it was like some invisible force held my boat in a stationary position. My headlamp caught a man in the throes of terror, his eyes wide with fear, as his kayak was forced into a narrow channel of trees. The boat got snared by a giant tree limb and began to fill with water. Dick had no other option than to abandon the craft. He found himself standing waist-deep in the muddy waters of the river.

The current pushed the boat, which was now upside down under a tree limb. It was impossible for Dick to pull the craft out until he wadded down and pulled it from the other side of the tree. That's when the Bell Witch claimed another soul. As Dick wadded down to pull the boat out, he began to disappear very slowly into the river. My mind couldn't comprehend the situation. Then it came to me that Dick was caught in quicksand. Dick was by then chest-deep in the water, screaming at the top of his lungs. Bart and John tried to paddle to help him, but the same invisible force held them motionless. All we could do was watch as the river swallowed him whole. His head slowly disappeared beneath the surface, his screams silenced forever. After a few seconds, his arm suddenly broke the surface, and I will never forget the blood dripping off his hand as if something was eating him alive! The force that held our kayaks released us, and we paddled over to the spot where Dick had disappeared, Bart was very emotional. He yelled out in anger, "Come on, your old bitch. Show yourself!" As soon as he spoke those words, I heard eerie laughter near the cave. There was no sign of Dick List, so Bart quoted a few words from the Bible, trying to neutralize the evil that we all felt. As we paddled away from the underwater resting place of Dick List, I looked over at Vicki, her face very pale. I could see the fear in her eyes. I wanted to hold her, to gently touch her, and kiss her face gently, but there was no time for that, so I turned my kayak downstream and whispered a prayer, praising the Creator of the universe for allowing us to survive the evil of the night.

CHAPTER 3

As we paddled, Judge would growl now and then, but he did not move a muscle, traumatized by the ordeal that he witness Dick List suffer. I could see the sun begin the rise, its orange rays beginning to penetrate the countryside. Bart began to maneuver his kayak to the shore, waving his mammoth arm and beckoning us to duplicate his path. When we all reached the shore, Bart directed us to a small arch made of sandstone. He explained that the Red River Gorge had over one hundred arches and land bridges carved by the river over a million-year time span. Bart instructed each of us to apply the cloaking lotion on our bodies, adding that the lotion would cover any body-heat signature, so the Annunaki heat-seeking scanners would not pick up our location.

"These ships are invisible to the naked eye because the Annunaki have an advanced cloaking mechanism. This is our itinerary for the day. We will set up camp underneath the protective covering of the arch. All tents will be set in a linear formation. I will set the command tent in the middle. At 1000 hours, breakfast will be served; at 1200 hours a command meeting will convene in the command ten. Attendance is mandatory. Finally, sleep hours will be between 1300 and 1800 hundred hours. Shaun, you and Judge will take the first two hours of the watch; Vicki and Blackjack will take the last four hours. Are there any questions?" he asked eyeing us all, daring anyone to have the audacity to make a rude commentary. So, I, being the only nonconformist, asked, "Excuse me head honcho, when did I sign up for military induction?" I half expected Bart to bite my head off.

"The same time that I was given the responsibility to save your life, and it's a commitment that I take very seriously, Shaun," Bart replied with a flash of resentment in his eyes.

The meeting was adjoined, and Vicki and I left to set up our tents side by side, if the commander in chief approved. Trying to impress Vicki with my knowledge of geology and geography, I informed her that arches are formed by water and wind erosion. She turned and calmly replied, "Ah, Shaun, you forgot that the downward pressure of gravity strengths and compresses some areas, leaving pillars after the wind or water consumes the more vulnerable portions."

"Well. excuse me for my incompetence, Professor Jenkins." We both laughed, and when she looked at me, the rising sun illuminated the irises of her eyes which for a second shined with a brilliant color that was not of this world.

"It's okay, grasshopper, now get over it so I can rub this magic lotion on your back, and you can return the favor. We don't want to disappoint the commander and chief." We both laughed like a couple of lunatics.

We enjoyed a breakfast of cold oatmeal and fruit because Bart explained that a campfire would be too risky with the Annunaki searching for us. I decided to take Judge for a brief walk, allowing him to expend some energy, before the command meeting at noon or 1200 hours.

"Ms. Jenkins, would you like to accompany us?" I asked and she accepted without reservation. As we departed the camping area, Daddy Bart instructed us not to stray far in case we had to depart abruptly.

As we talked along the edge of the river, I was so transfixed by the beauty of the steep sandstone cliffs that formed the canyons above us, I didn't notice Vicki begin to weep. It was contagious because I had begun the grieving process for my newly departed aunt and uncle and my best friend Pee Wee. The tears soon transformed into uncontrollable sobs as the sadness, guilt, and anger escaped my heart. Vicki turned and hugged me with an intensity and love that confirmed the theory that she indeed was my soulmate. We stood locked in an embrace that allowed us to escape this horrifying reality. We were conjoined in grief that we both shared, forming a bond that only pain and loss could create. When the pain subsided, I turned her face to mine and kissed her with an intensity born out of empathy and compassion, instead of sexuality. We stood there in each other's arms for what seemed an eternity--until Judge's barking broke the spell. He was upset because I hadn't bent down to retrieve the stick that I had thrown earlier so that he could work on his hunting skills while on vacation.

"Good boy," I said as I patted his head with love, knowing that he along with Vicki were the only reasons that I still wanted to exist. I looked at Vicki and calmly asked her what time it was. She glanced at the cell phone, omnipresent in modern times.

"It's 11:55, and we are going to be late for the dreaded command meeting," she said, her eyes wide with mock fear.

We walked back at a quickened pace, trying desperately to stifle our emotions. Vicki slowed and then asked me a weird question.

"Shaun, do you ever think about the karma of the universe? Do you think we will face negative karma because of our betrayal of Pee Wee?" Her voice was filled with emotion and grief.

"I don't know, Vicki. We have all sinned. However, we are forgiven by the blood of Christ," I replied, sounding like a third-year student at a Bible college. "Why do you ask?"

"Well, Shaun, since we are on a camping trip, well kind of, I have a ghost story to tell you. I hope it doesn't frighten you too much. There is a house on the corner of Main Street and Nashville Road in Russellville. It has a large cemetery behind it. The Sexton House is on America's Most Haunted Places list, and it's definitely not an urban legend," Vicki said, defending her position, seeming to be reacting to my "your nuts" expression.

"Vicki, so the haunted house is built on a cemetery. Mr. Sexton deserves everything he gets for building his home on ghost central," I said, laughing.

"Shaun, 'sexton' is an old-fashion term for a caretaker of a cemetery, so please no further interruptions: it's better for someone to think you're ignorant than to open your mouth and erase all doubt." She let the last remark linger in the air to emphasize her point.

"The house has a tower that faces Ninth Street. Many of the historical houses in Russellville have the same architectural design, so it seems to be a fashion statement of the time. The tale begins with a young girl who became upset because a sudden thunderstorm had ruined her date with a young man that had struck her fancy. She began to curse God in angry, violent words and was, at that very moment stuck by lightning and killed."

On the risk of being thought of as ignorant, I interjected, "Well, excuse me, that's not too scary. Just your average fit of adolescent rage and rebellion."

"Your absolutely correct, Shaun, except that most rebellious teenagers don't have their ghostly image projected onto a window for all eternity. On stormy nights, the girl's image appears in that very window, her defiance and anger at God frozen in time as a lesson for those tempted to swear at God."

"Wow, after all this is over, you will have to show me this ghostly masterpiece of supernatural art," I said with a faked look of terror.

"Make fun, Shaun! Unfortunately, you won't be able to see the image in the window because they painted over the window to prevent accidents at that intersection in Russellville. Many tourists would come to Russellville to gawk at the house after the site was made famous and gained notoriety."

We were almost at the tent when she turned and looked at me with fear and pain in her eyes. That fear made me want to hug her close, but I couldn't understand how a story that she had known for years had upset her so much at this time. Then she asked me a question that would be of great relevance later that night.

"Shaun, what if we are like the girl in the window? Will our actions of betrayal cause us to experience negative karma? Do we have a target on our backs, Shaun?" Her eyes were as large and round, but there was no time to answer her insightful question because we were already late for the command meeting.

As we entered the tent at approximately 12:05 and were greeted by the stares of our companions, the awkwardness of the situation was compounded by the extremely cramped conditions in the tent. Bart stared at us for what seemed to be an eternity, but to his credit, he didn't say a word. I assumed that he could tell by our expressions that grief and sadness about our loved ones had delayed our attendance. He nodded his head as if to say, "I understand your grief!"

He cleared his throat, and said, "Shaun, I need that cell phone that is linked to the listening device was planted in the home of the Annunaki leader." He didn't mention any names or that the Annunaki leader was my stepfather. That indicated that he wanted to help me created an emotional detachment from the alien that had posed as my stepfather for years.

"Think you can get any reception in this remote area? I didn't see any cell towers close by."

"Shaun, that is why John chose this device; it can pick up that phone charger listening device anywhere in the world," Bart said slowly as if he were speaking to a child. He dialed the number to the listening device that was planted in the alien leader's library. There was a brief static, but then a voice that I recognized immediately came through my generation 7 iPhone.

"I want my stepson located and exterminated yesterday!" Mad Dog screamed into the phone.

A voice, sounding a lot like President Tweet, identified itself as the reptilian representative of the United States. "I have ordered every federal law enforcement agency including the C.I.A., F.B.I., and Homeland Security to track him down. I have put his picture on every social media site and on C.N.N., FOX, and other large news affiliates across the country. He is being listed on the F.B.I.'s America's Most Wanted List as a domestic terrorist. I expect that we will either apprehend or kill him within the next few hours." The obedient voice of the Commander-in-chief of the free world droned on like a programmed cyborg. I cleared my throat, as a tension reliever, and we all continued to listen to a conference call to reptilian leaders around the globe.

"I hope, for your sake, he is captured or killed by the next time we speak. I have some grave concerns to address today but being the supreme leader of the Annunaki on earth, I have a three-step solution. The data presented to me by our leading scientists on our home planet

Nibiru suggest that our beloved planet will explode with the supernova in less than a year in Earth time. Our attempt to change the climate and life-sustaining environment on Earth has made great progress. Through deforestation and slash and burn agriculture, we have decreased the chemical process of photosynthesis, thus decreasing the oxygen supply on a planet already starving for clean air.

We have also increased the carbon dioxide emissions by burning fossil fuels and combined with the release of methane gas through hydraulic fracturing, we have increased the average global temperatures by ten degrees. This temperature increase had caused the ice caps to melt, increasing the flooding threat to coastal areas. Global warming has presented many problematic areas for the human species, including creating monster hurricanes, powerful tornados, drought, and wildfires. Hell! We have even torn a hole in the ozone layer above the Antarctic Circle. Before you slap each other on the back, I submit that we have run out of time and must resort to another strategy." Mad Dog Alien paused for a moment and slammed his fist down on the desk. The looks on our group's faces ranged from intense anger to horrified disbelief.

The alien bastard paused for a moment, then offered his plan to expedite the demise of the human species.

"First, I have activated our Manchurian Candidate in Wuhan, China, to release a virus that will deadly to humans. It will be airborne and extremely contagious. All Annunaki and reptilian brothers will be completely immune to the virus. It will cause a pandemic that encircles the globe within a year's time. Second, we will create a great fear that causes social isolation. That will create anxiety and increase mental stress, making the sheep easy to control. We will dehumanize them. No touching. No weddings. No parties. Churches and places of spiritual growth will be closed, so they can worship Big Brother and elements of Big Government, which are our puppets. We will cause financial and economic hardships in the most prosperous countries, thus undermining their currency systems around the globe. Finally, we will create perceived social injustice to ignite hatred and civil war with great unrest. Armed citizens will kill the innocent. We will create hate groups bent on undermining the ideological concepts of democracy and erasing it by looting, burning, and defacing monuments and statues, thus eliminating "By the people, and for the people forever."

You, reptilian leaders, will speak in doubletalk and half-truths, mumbling asinine concepts like "War is peace." Your press releases will be rich with alternative facts, and you will use the Internet to spread conspiracy theories, fake news, and other dogma. We will insert malware into the financial markets and electronic grids of the major superpowers like China, Russia, and the United States. These superpowers will increase aggressive military action, heightening the probability of nuclear war. Finally, the Intelligence agencies of the superpowers will use spyware to rig elections in other countries and will use deep fake-technology to cause an Armageddon. In the end, the human species will exterminate themselves in mass genocide. We will then convert any survivors to cyborgs, using them as warriors to expand our presence in the galaxy. So, like the British in the 1800s, the sun will never set on the Annunaki empire!"

There was dead silence after the plan was detailed, and seconds later, we heard several voices unified as one utter the word "Genius!" We all sat in stunned silence, as the brilliant strategy was revealed, and I began to wonder how my extraction was going to help humanity stop the evil that was speeding at them like a runaway train.

CHAPTER 4

I got back to my tent just in time for my two-hour watch. Bart had set up a chair under the arch. The sturdy outdoor canvas chair was near the northern side of the arch and had a 360-degree view of the perimeter. Bart handed me some binoculars that were extremely high-tech.

"These bad boys have a range of 2,800 yards and a magnification of 7, so try not to lose them, Hoss." He winked and entered the command tent, confident that his proxy would stay alert and ready for action. Vicki walked up, gave me a hug, and a quick peck on the check.

She then whispered quietly, "You're my hero, Shaun, and I think that I am falling in love with you."

I turned to make sure that I wasn't having an auditory hallucination, and she had already walked off toward her tent. Her sweet scent still lingered in the air, and I felt that I had been visited by an angel. I put the binoculars up to my eyes and scanned the ancient river and surrounding terrain. The binoculars were so powerful that I could have seen a worm grin on a fisherman's baited hook. I watched the sunrise in the east and began to think of the Annunaki's diabolical plan. My hand began to tremble, thinking of how my fellow human beings were living their last days in complete oblivion to their impending doom.

As I sat guarding the camp, I began thinking of how ninety-five percent of the Earth's population followed automatic patterns in their lives. They were like sleepwalkers or zombies in a protected matrix. Those that are "awake" are classified as crazies who spouted conspiracy theories, but they were the enlightened ones. We were all like the heroes in one of my favorite movies, *The Matrix* with Keanu Reeves. Yea! That's it. I'm as cool as Keanu Reeves, and I laughed out loud at my vanity, but deep down it was lonely being the last Soul Searcher on Earth. The enormous pressure to save humanity was almost a burden that crushed my soul. I might get extracted and forget all about my responsibilities, Ah, shit, deep down I knew that I would protect humanity with my last dying breath. I knew that the heart that beat in my chest was not capable of deserting my species.

The sound of the current was almost as relaxing as the crashing of the waves on some exotic beach. It lulled me into a semiconscious state. I always thought that nature was God's therapy for stress and anxiety. It was His cosmic antidepressant. When Vicki put her hand on my shoulder, I almost jumped out of my skin!

"Hey, dereliction of duty, sailor, sleeping on duty. Bart will have you court-marshaled and horse-whipped," Vicki said with a huge grin on her exquisite face.

I defended myself by retorting, "I was just dreaming of your beautiful face."

I got up in a hurry. My arms were aching from the twelve hours of paddling, but I managed to kiss her lips as I stumbled off to my sleeping bag, which had the added luxury of a blow-up mattress. I tossed and turned all day, and just when I fell asleep, Blackjack's big head peered into my tent.

"Time to get up. Bart is having evening prayer before casting off," he bellowed, and the sound of his voice was more effective than any alarm clock. I felt that I had not slept at all. I was drowsy, my arms ached, and I had an ugly premonition that tonight's trip was going to end in tragedy.

As I packed my kayak, a strong wind blew out of the northeast. The moon's rays streamed down upon the river, and I noticed that the current was faster, so I whispered to my best buddy Judge, "Be very still tonight, my friend, and maybe, just maybe, we will survive the night."

Judge looked at me and whimpered, not because he was frightened, but because it was dinner time, and he was starving. I walked over to the others, feeding Judge some stale potato chips along the way. I arrived in time to hear Reverend Bart ask the Lord to protect us from the evils of the Annunaki. After hearing the plans that my alien stepfather had for humanity, it was safe to say that we would need all the divine intervention we could get. After the blessing, Bart, in all his religious glory, shouted somewhat sacrilegiously, "Now get your asses in the boats. We have a great distance to travel."

I walked over to Vicki, hugged her, and asked her how she slept.

She winked at me and said, "I would have slept much better in your arms!" I then understood what the sleeping arrangements would be tomorrow, and I was suddenly motivated and energized.

We used the same box formation as the day before, minus one Dick List, who was now fish bait. Thank God that the wind was at our back, so the current and the wind carried us quickly downriver. We paddled with just the moonlight illuminating our way. I was on automatic pilot paddling with strength and endurance that seemed to come from a supernatural source. Perhaps the Arcturians were propelling me toward my destiny. The night went smoothly, until after the second rally point. Blackjack warned us that we would be entering some class-two rapids. They would drop the kayaks down about a foot overall.

"Listen, folks. You're going to have to watch me. If you see me paddle on the right, then you do that. Copy my movements quickly and exactly. We are going to tighten the box, so the trailing kayak will be about ten feet behind me. Blackjack will be in the lead, and I will be replicating his every move." Bart's voice was stern and serious.

I approached the rapids with trepidation, feeling that my worst fear was going to come true. The kayak increased in speed, almost at the mercy of the current. Rocks and boulders turned the gentle river into a vicious beast, almost like a bipolar person made changing moods, shocking even to their loved ones. I followed Bart's movements like an adjoined twin, and just when I thought we would come out unscathed, Judge jumped to one side of the kayak, causing me to be off-balance just when I had cleared the last rock. The kayak began to fill with water. Then it capsized in the swirling current, throwing Judge and me into the cold waters. When I finally surfaced, Judge was nowhere to be found. I began to yell his name, but my cries of pain and anguish were muffled by the wind.

I flipped on my headlamp, violating Bart's orders, and swept the beam downstream, hoping to spot one of my companions holding my long-time friend. Tears welled up in my eyes. I was blinded by fear and felt deep remorse for bringing Judge along as I realized that Judge's and Dick List's souls had been claimed by this evil river. I turned my face toward the heavens and for the second time in my life, howled at God with the intensity of a demon straight from the bowels of hell. I began to swim with an intensity of a madman, trying to catch up to my dog wherever he was. As I was propelled down the river, a muscular arm wrapped around my torso with a power and force that seemed to be superhuman. It was Bart, and like a human towboat, he was pulling me toward a small island. I screamed at him to let me go and began to fight with all the strength that I could muster.

All I heard was Bart's strong masculine voice say, "I sure hate to do this, Hoss," and then nothing but a smothering blackness as my brain slipped into unconsciousness.

When I regained consciousness, John and Jack were emptying river water out of my kayak using the water plug in the back of the boat. I watched as they took my wet gear out and placed it on the beach. They were using some type of heating device to dry my gear.

My jaw was aching, and I suddenly knew that Bart had hit me. Anger and fury erupted, and I got to my feet prepared to bum rush the bastard who had stopped me from rescuing my buddy Judge. As I began to run toward Bart, a hand stopped my advance. I swirled ready to fight to the death.

"Stop, Shaun, Bart had no other choice than to hit you. You were out of your mind in grief, and your actions were putting both your lives in danger," Vicki yelled in my ear. The sound of her voice was like a sedative impacting my central nervous system. I turned and hugged her with the intensity of a burning volcano. I was sobbing and kept repeating Judge's name repeatedly. I then realized that the karma that I had so richly deserved had finally caught up with me.

CHAPTER 5

It was two o'clock in the morning. We still had about four hours of paddling ahead of us. I did not have proper time to grief Judge. It was time to cowboy up, so I walked over and thanked Blackjack and John for draining my boat and drying my gear. They both looked at me with sympathy, and John placed his hand on my shoulder as if he was trying to drain my body of pain through osmosis. I nodded my head, and Bart came up and apologized for hitting me. The expression on his face confirmed that he was terribly sorry. He held out his giant hand; and knowing we didn't have time for grudges on this trip, I shook it in solidarity.

We paddled in silence for the next three hours. The wind was howling, and the trees were swaying in the wind, dead, decaying leaves rustling. The sound of the leaves seemed like an omen, warning us not to proceed on this suicide mission. I was numb, not from the wind, but from the pain of losing three people I dearly loved and my faithful, loyal companion. I paddled on like a zombie or some other creature with an empty heart. The tears stung my eyes, and I was glad that I was alone in the night.

We finally reached our resting area at a place called Princess Arch. I dragged my gear to the arch and set up camp. Bart had given out watch times, and I was relieved that I was not included on the watch team. The combination of grief compounded with no sleep had robbed me of strength. I crawled into my tent and collapsed into an exhaustive slumber.

I was shocked a couple of hours later when a warm body lay down beside me. I didn't even turn to check who it was. I was just hoping it wasn't Bart trying to cuddle me after clearing showing the group who the alpha male was. I will never forget what happened next. A fierce growl echoed through the tent. I turned to see Vicki's beautiful face. Her eyes open after hearing the ruckus that was taking place about fifteen feet from our tent. He both got up quickly, the cool air rushing in as we opened our camouflaged tent flap. Outside Bart was circling a deranged black bear.

The bear was foaming at the mouth and clearly rabid. It was on its hind legs, its large eyes bulging out their sockets, its huge claws and teeth ready to rip Bart into pieces. It was over seven feet tall, and its fur was matted with blood. I then noticed that Bart had a gash on his left arm. I started to make noises to get the bear's attention, but it was too late. The bear dropped to all fours and charged Bart like he was a matador in a bullfight.

The events that followed were so incredible that they would be burned into my brain forever. Bart waited for the bear to close within ten feet. He then crouched down, his legs filled with kinetic energy ready to be released. With a speed that was indeed superhuman, he jumped over the bear's head and landed on its back. He then locked his arms around the bear's neck and snapped its neck like a chicken bone. I was shocked to witness a man kill a huge black bear with his bare hands when I saw Bart's wounds close and heal by themselves!

I stared at him for a couple of minutes, and he looked over at me and calmly said, "Hello, Hoss. Make sure you and your filly are not late for the command meeting in an hour." Vicki and I nodded our heads. In complete shock, we both looked at each other as the same thought entered our brains at the same time: who or what are we trusting our lives with. I was suddenly aware of my thoughts. First, I was so glad Vicki stopped me from attacking this man. It would have been pure suicide. Second, I was suddenly very glad that I was going to be extracted that night.

CHAPTER 6

Vicki and I were five minutes early for the command meeting, and we were full of questions for our leader. Bart wanted me to dial the spy device that I had planted in my alien daddy's library. I truly was hating to have to hear that bastard's voice again. The phone made the connection to the charger, and there was nothing for almost five minutes. I then heard the human voice of a creature cloaked in its man-suit.

"I have been informed by President Tweet that Shaun, the Arcturian pawn, is traveling with an assassin that has been killing our reptilian brothers for twenty years. He is an Army special forces lieutenant in the first Iraqi Conflict. Single-handedly, he killed fifty members of Saddam Hussein's elite Republican Guard. For his heroism under fire, he was awarded the Medal of Honor. After the war, he was recruited by every covert government organization from the Central Intelligence Agency to the Federal Bureau of Investigation. He chose to work with an organization so secretive that only the top brass knew of its existence. It was an offshoot of the Air Force's Project Bluebook, and its main function was to assassinate any high-ranking government officials that were suspected of not being human. He knew our vulnerabilities and created weapons that would exploit our weaknesses. He was amazingly effective in killing our reptilian brothers until about five years ago. An operational ambush designed by our reptilian operatives captured him and five others.

We killed his peers. But the Annunaki converted this seriously wounded killer into a cyborg--part human, part killing machine. He had been killing our rivals in other galaxies when he escaped three years ago. He is extremely dangerous with superhuman strength and immunity to many weapons systems, both human and alien. He can heal any wounds and even regrow appendages if he needs to."

Bart disconnected the call. There was an awkward silence in the tent. We just could not believe that our leader was part machine, but we were even more concerned about where his loyalties lay. Could he be leading us into an ambush? Bart was silent for a few minutes.

Then he spoke in a low serious voice, "Everything you have heard is true. I was an Annunaki cyborg, killing indiscriminately and without mercy for three years, but do not fear me. I have been reprogrammed by the Arcturians after they rescued me, and because of my knowledge of the Annunaki, I have been chosen by the Arcturian leadership to extract human resources that they deemed too valuable to lose. Shaun, you're my fifth extraction, so as I told you, this is not my first rodeo."

"Wait a damn minute. This is insane. You seem so human--a bit deranged and weird--but human. So, let me get this straight, you are part human and part machine? Are you like Yul Brynner, who played robotic gunslinger in the movie *Westworld*?" I asked, hoping that Bart would not take any offense. Bart paused for a moment, then he spoke, and his answer gave me the internal peace I was seeking.

"Shaun, I was born human. My spirit will always be human, like yours. My body was riddled with bullets, so they replaced my lungs, liver, and most of my abdominal cavity with alien parts, then they brainwashed me to believe that I owed them my complete allegiance. It took the Arcturians a year to free me from the mental bondage of the Annunaki.

"Shaun, I am human because my first instinct will always be to save humanity. I would rather serve an eternity in hell than let the Annunaki capture or kill you!"

As he spoke these words, he rose to his feet, his eyes ablaze with emotion, his fist in the air. Damn, I was fired up like it was halftime in the locker room and we were down by a touchdown. I put my hand on his back and told him that I trusted him with my life.

He then turned to me with a tear in his eye and said, "Then let's get 'er done, Hoss." Then he laughed. The laughter sounded purely human, not at all robotic.

Bart redialed the number to the listening device, and we all very shocked to learn that the Annunaki knew exactly where the extraction point was.

"President Tweet has a team in the Red River Gorge area, in the proximity of Natural Bridge, an arch that spans the sandstone canyon. My research team informed me that there is a ninety-percent chance that the extraction of my stepson will take place in that rugged area. The height and angle of the bridge are perfect for the Arcturian extraction. Our meteorological experts believe that the extraction will take place tonight. Weather conditions include light wind, lunar Illumination with no cloud cover. Perfect for an extraction. Specialized teams that have been conditioned to survive in limited toxic areas have been dispatched to that area with orders to terminate every one of those rebellious bastards."

The phone then became mysterious silent, as if we had lost the connection.

Bart was silent, his large cranium wrinkled in deep thought. The confident air of enthusiasm and positivity seemed to have left his body.

"Listen, folks. Time to change to Plan B, an extraction is now going to be at Seventy Six Falls near Albany, Kentucky. It is not my first choice. In fact, if it were not an emergency, I would not even attempt it, but you know what they say--desperate times call for desperate measures."

Both Vicki and I said in unison, "We have already been there!"

I was in shock. It was like cosmic forces were showing us the place where we would perish. Those days before were our getting a preview of the place that would be critically important to us. I was now a firm believer in déjà vu. I only wished now that I had a vision of how future events were going to turn out.

Bart just looked at us, and said, "Great! Your familiarity with the place just might help you survive."

I glanced at Vicki and had to address the elephant in the room. "What makes that area so problematic?"

"Many reasons, Shaun. First, the Natural Bridge provided cover that is completed exposed at Seventy Six Falls, making the Arcturian craft assisting in the extraction very vulnerable to an Annunaki ambush. Second, the angle of incidence for the extraction is off by about five percent, meaning that the Arcturian extraction beams may miss you completely. Lastly, if the beams do miss you, you will drop one hundred feet to the bottom of the falls where the currents and the undertow will drown you if you're not already dead from the drop."

I had to ask another critical question, "Have you ever tried this location before for an extraction?" A slight tremor shook my voice.

And without even the slightest batting of his eyes, Bart replied, "Yea, it was a complete and utter failure, both folks died a horrible death with bodies burned beyond recognition."

I looked at Vicki. Her face was very pale, and her expression said it all--that she didn't sign up for this shit. Bart paused for a moment, letting the tension build.

Then the damn cyborg thing said, "Ah, I was just bullshitting you. Damn! Wish you could have seen the expressions on your faces." His loud and arrogant chuckles cause several ducks to take flight in terror. I shook my head and then laughed. In fact, we all started giggling like a bunch of Girl Scouts around a campfire. It somewhat eased my pain after losing Judge, but it was just temporary. Soon a cold chill ran down my back as I thought of Pee Wee, my Aunt Jackie, and Uncle Jim. I wondered if this extraction was another change in the universe and if karma would deal me the fate that I so richly deserved.

CHAPTER 7

"The jump has to very precise. Quantum physics. Longitude and latitude. Meteorological data, like the Coriolis effect and wind speed. They are all considered in an extraction. We will meet at a rally point five miles from the falls. I will be in contact with the Arcturians during the last segment of our trip, finalizing the exact details. We should arrive at Seventy Six Falls by 0400. John and I will set up the defense perimeters around Indian Creek, a tributary that branches off the Red River, and is the source of the water of the falls," Bart explained as he closed out the command meeting. Any questions?" Bart asked as we were all walking toward the kayaks, which were arranged in the wedge formation.

"Yea, so what if the calculations are wrong or we jump at the wrong time or from the wrong point?" I asked silently hoping that he would lie to me.

"Well, Shaun, have you ever watched movies about space capsules trying to re-enter Earth's atmosphere at the wrong speed or angle?"

"Let me interject here, Bart. N.A.S.A. nearly miscalculated the reentry speeds of *Apollo 14,* which would have caused the capsule to disintegrate above the Indian Ocean," Vicki whispered.

I looked at Vicki and was horrified to think that we might pay the ultimate sacrifice in our noble efforts to save mankind.

She smiled and then winked at me and asked, "If only I had brought my fire-retardant suit?" I laughed trying to appear to be Mr. Macho, but I was petrified to the core. As I pushed the kayak into the Red River, I glanced at the back compartment and my heart ached for Judge, but I checked my emotions and began to paddle with a fury that would assist me in ignoring my emotions.

There was a slight wind gently pushing us downstream. The moonlight brilliantly reflected off the water and seemed to light our path in a golden, almost supernatural water trail. I missed my companion. My eyes misted over, but I kept paddling and prayed that the next set of silvery eyes peering from the shoreline would be those of my faithful, loyal dog.

We were nearing the Indian Creek tributary. We had to paddle hard to the left to escape the currents of the river. We all managed the turn, and Bart signaled that the rally point would be five hundred yards downstream.

"It is exactly 0400. The Arcturians set your jump time at 0500. Shaun, you and Vicki must jump between 0459 and 0501. If you are earlier or later, your bodies will be caught between dimensions and disintegrate. The Arcturians have specified that your jump will be at 36.77916 degrees west, and 85.12591 degrees north. They have marked that area with a glowing white rock underneath the water. This area will be under Indian Creek as it flows off the abyss into Cumberland Lake. John Running Bull, Blackjack, and I will set up the defense perimeter exactly 500 yards from the jump point.

"Indian Creek becomes shallow a quarter of a mile from the falls. We will have to ditch the kayaks and walk the rest of the way. Listen, your job is to find that rock and leap precisely at the exact time. Do not turn around to check on us no matter what you hear! Do you understand? God and the Arcturians will protect you!"

He was very animated and spoke with a great passion. At that moment, I looked at my mentor and great friend John Running Bull, his eyes radiated love and admiration that I will take to the grave.

He said, "I am very proud of you, my son. And I will see you someday in the Happy Hunting Grounds."

It was almost like he was predicting his death, but I didn't have time to get a clarification. I merely said, "Love you, dude. You have been like a father to me."

"Enough of this sentimental shit. We are running out of time," Bart screamed, recovering from his moment of weakness.

After the rally point, Vicki and I assumed the lead positions, and John, Bart, and Jack assumed the defensive positions to our rear. Indian Creek narrowed and was so shallow that our kayaks kept hitting the rocky bottom of the creek. We ditched them on the grassy banks of the creek. Vicki and I checked our waterproofed watches that Bart had given us. It was 0440, so we started to run toward the falls. My heart and lungs were pulsating with fear intertwined excitement. I looked at Vicki. Her eyes were wide, nostrils flared with heated passion. God forgive me because I was slightly aroused. Because the year had been dry, the current was very weak, and the water was barely trickling over the edge.

Once we reached the edge, I checked the compass. We were just a few degrees off on both longitude and latitude coordinates. I was so busy looking for the white luminous rock that I didn't hear the first explosions of the laser beams as they filled the air. It was 0455 when I turned to look upstream. What I saw filled me with both wonder and terror.

A blur of white and tan fur was running with a pace that was born of a love to be reunited with his master. Judge was on the opposite side of the bank along the fence that kept tourists and crazies away from the ledge.

Bart was running toward us, and even though he was a great distance from us, I thought I heard him yell, "Don't jump! It's an ambush."

I gasped and cried out in horror when both Blackjack and my mentor were liquefied by direct hits of gamma rays. The rays just bouncing off Bart as he was returning fire with his own piece of Annunaki killing technology.

"Shaun, it's 0459. We have to jump," Vicki shouted almost crying with fear as she looked over the edge of the cliff. I turned to look at Judge. He was only twenty-five feet away. I yelled at him, "Come on, boy!"

His face was transfixed in a Herculean effort, spittle dripping off his chin, eyes bulging with a look of fierceness and determination of an Olympic athlete. I took one more look upstream and saw Mad Dog MacGregor, the beast, pointing a weapon at Bart. He fired. The projectile struck Bart in the chest. He twitched, his mouth and nose exploded with a bright stream of red blood, and then the impossible happened. The invincible one collapsed into the stream. His blood seeped downstream in the turbulence of the water, now stained a cloudy crimson.

I did not have time to process it all. I looked at my watch it was 0500. We only had ten seconds, then five seconds left, when Judge jumped into my arms. I grabbed Vicki's hand and we jumped!

Suddenly, we were falling. The wind was hitting my face. Then the wind suddenly stopped, and we were in a tunnel with a bright light at the end. It was remarkably--like what people recall in near-death experiences. I heard Judge whimpering and could not feel Vicki's hand. The wormhole began to close. I could not breathe. My lungs were screaming for air. I heard a faint explosion, and the lights I saw turned into the colors of a vibrant rainbow. The tunnel began to pulsate as if we were pushing out of a birth canal. The pressure was forcing us through an invisible boundary.

I began to lose consciousness, and my last thought before everything went black was that karma had finally caught up to me.

PART 3
Living the Dream

●━◆━●

Mid- to Late October 1956
Brentwood, Tennessee

Chapter 1

I woke up to Elvis Presley accusing someone of being nothing but a hound dog, and I thought that some lame rock and roll station was playing a blast from the past. I opened my eyes and turned to the source of the assault on my hearing. I saw an old Zenith Model AM/FM radio. Of course, it had no snooze button. I tried to locate the power switch and could not. So, I grabbed the radio and threw it against the wall. After that, I noticed an old antique R.C.A. black and white television sitting at the front of the bed.

"What the hell?" I thought and began to look around the room. It was like being a guest on *Storage Wars*, the television series that had participants bid on abandoned storage units. It looked like I got ripped off because the furniture in this bedroom was straight out of the 1950s.

It was still very dark in the room. Quickly, I did a mental inventory: my name is Shaun MacGregor; I am the last soul searcher on earth; I jumped off an eighty-foot waterfall. Yep, all my mental facilities are in place, and then all my memories came flooding back to me like they were being downloaded from some giant computer. I had to urinate urgently, so I swung my legs to the side of the bed and waddled off to the bathroom which was conveniently adjoining the bedroom as one might expect. I did my business and washed my face, trying to cope with my new reality.

Then I looked in the mirror and got the shock of my life. I was peering at an impostor. The face staring back at me looked purely Italian--with a cheesy mustache. My pale white complexion and Scots-Irish features were replaced by a man who looked exactly like Mario--as in the video game. I had an olive complexion, dark curly hair, and a bushy mustache. My eyes emitted a sparkle and a zest for life, which suggest hot and passionate Italian blood flowing through my veins.

I returned to the bedroom and received two more shocks. In a full-length mirror, I was horrified to a rather diminutive, pudgy man, rather than the 6'3" broad-shouldered specimen that I was before the jump. I looked back at the be. Tucked away under the covers, breathing ever so slightly, was an Ivory-skinned woman with bright red hair. "Oh, please, let that be Vicki and not some hooker that I picked up in the tunnel connecting the two dimensions," I thought strangely. I was going to shake the woman to confirm that she was indeed my love who had survived the jump with me, but before I could move, I noticed an envelope lying on the dresser. It had **Shaun** written in bold letters. It read:

"Hey, Shaun, old Hoss, if you are reading this letter, then I gave my life to make sure you and Vicki were safe and sound. Now, old Hoss, don't shed any tears for me. I was ready to go to that giant rodeo in the sky. I wanted to give you these instructions in person, but the damn Annunaki had other plans. Here's what you absolutely must know in your new life.

"Do absolutely nothing to draw attention to yourself as a time traveler.

"Vicki is employed at Vanderbilt Hospital, as before, as a registered nurse. You, my friend, are a freight handler at the shed at Union Station, the train station.

"In the drawer are Social Security cards, Tennessee Drivers Licenses, and birth certificates for both of you. A checkbook is also there with a joint account for you two. You and Vicki are married now and have been living in Nashville for the past ten years, recently moving to the Brentwood area.

"Your names are now Angelo and Cassandra Francisco. You are in your late thirties, just as before. Cassandra is five years younger. You are both in perfect health. You have no cardiac issues at all, Shaun. You can thank me for that in the next life.

"You two moved from New York City where you met. You played rugby at Cornell. Vicki finished at the university with a bachelor's in nursing. You dropped out before finishing your degree after your sophomore year when you and Vicki were married in 1946.

"I also left you five thousand dollars in cash in the top of the cedar chest at the foot of the bed. I couldn't allow you to be homeless living in a cardboard box on Broadway. L.O.L. I put all these items in the room on my last time travel trip because my witness protection program is the envy of the galaxy.

"It was an honor to help you, Shaun--uh, Angelo. I hope that you will remember me. If you're ever hiking in the mountains on a misty morning and spot a brocken spectre with a halo of brilliant colors, it is me watching out for you, my friend. The Arcturians will be coming to recover you when and If the Annunaki threat is gone. Never forget me, John Running Bull, and Blackjack. Make sure the ultimate price we paid is not in vain."

Tears welled up in my eyes, and I began to cry, in both pain and sadness. So much loss and death. My crying woke up Vicki, now Cassandra. She got out of bed and wrapped her arms around me. I then knew that my eternal soulmate had survived the jump and that her beautiful soul was still intact.

Vicki noticed her new look in the full-length mirror and asked me, "Do I look more like Julianne Moore or Nicole Kidman?" batting her beautiful emerald-colored eyes.

"Baby, you are Cassandra Francisco, my exotically beautiful wife," I said showing her the note that Bart had left for us.

"Shaun, this is surreal. You think we are sharing some type of psychotic break? Or could this be a past-life experience born out of trauma?" Vicki's green eyes were ablaze with passion.

"I don't know, Vicki. Why don't you pinch me so I can determine if this is a dream or not?" I said hoping that a good dose of humor would alleviate the stress we were both feeling.

"Shaun, I have something else in mind to test your senses. The note from Bart said we were married, didn't it? So why don't we experience some marital relations?" she asked with a seductive wink. I was so surprised by her question that I didn't notice that her nipples were erect and very noticeable under her nightgown, tantalizing me with their seduction.

We made love with wild abandon like two souls joined after generations of separation. Vicki's orgasm was strong, she made sounds like a wild Irish banshee. Her approval of my manhood awakened a miniature poodle that came into the room and jumped in the bed with us with an extreme look of curiosity. We paused, embarrassed by our canine observer.

At the same time, we both yelled out "Judge?" He started licking our faces with great affection. Then, we both started laughing, and poor Judge turned his head sideways, trying desperately to understand what was so funny.

I looked at Vicki and commented, "Looks like Judge is also sharing our complete break from reality.

She laughingly replied, "Shaun, we have to get rid of all the mirrors in the house or poor Judge will be traumatized by his undercover image." We both laughed like a couple of teenagers stoned on pot. I began to think that our regression in time might just be what we both needed.

CHAPTER 2

V icki and I were watching the news. The anchor was droning
on about Senator Joseph McCarthy and his witch hunt against
communist spies inside our government as well as in Hollywood.

I looked over and said, "Kind of reminds me of President Tweet's
obsession with the folks south of the border. They were such a great
threat to the American way of life that we had to use billions of tax
dollars to build a fucking wall!"

"Sure, Shaun, kind of like the book by Tom Clancy, *Sum of All
Fears*. Everyone knows people are easier to control when they're in fear.
I think the Annunaki have used that strategy to control mankind for
years."

We ascertained was that the current date was Sunday, October 16,
1956. The news anchor also informed us that it had been a leap year.
Vicki and I laughed.

We looked at each other and said simultaneously, "No shit,
Sherlock!" We started to laugh like we were still stoned.

I used the old rotary phone on the nightstand and called the train
station and asked for their office. I wanted to get an idea of my work
schedule. The girl on the other line didn't ask for a password or social
security number. I guessed people trusted each other more in the fifties.
She told me that this week's schedule had me working the second
shift Monday through Friday. Vicki also checked on her schedule at
the hospital. She found out she was scheduled to work in the section
designated for newborn and premature babies. Given the baby boom of

the 1950s, we surmised she would be extremely busy. Finding out that we didn't have to report to our new jobs until Monday was welcomed news because we needed at least twenty-fours to acclimate to our new lives in a quite different world.

I was having trouble accepting this new reality. Was I dreaming, tucked away in my bed in the basement? Or was this really an alternate reality? Everything was so surreal. I looked down at my rather muscular frame and decided to take a short run, knowing full well that with my previous heart issues, it could possibly be my last run, but I had to test out my new body.

"Honey, going on a short run," I yelled as I headed out the front door, not wanting to hear any objections. I opened the door to a bright, crisp fall day. The first thing I noticed was Chevy Belair and a Mercury Montclair sitting in the driveway.

I thought, "Damn, being married to a beautiful, registered nurse is quite lucrative. I started running at a slow pace, fully expecting a deep, searing pain in my chest, but to my surprise, there was no pain. My body performed like a well-oiled machine. I started to run faster and thought this was the way someone feels when he enters the pearly gates of heaven in a new body. I ran for almost two miles, experiencing a release of endorphins I felt the often-mentioned runners' high.

I was walking back home, trying to cool down, and I noticed the homes of my neighbors, exceptionally clean and neat. Kids rode on Schwinn bikes. They were extremely respectful, wishing me a good day. All referred to me as sir. I was going to enjoy my time in this era. I noticed the street sign which read "Fugitive's Way." I smiled and thought that it very an appropriate name for a street I lived on.

The lawns were immaculate, manicured, and devoid of leaves. I saw many teenagers raking leaves and playing outside. It dawned on me that they had no video games like *Call of Duty* or Madden football, so they were outside getting fresh air and being active. I guess that's why teenager suicide was unheard of in this happy, family-focused era.

By the time I got home, I was beaming with enthusiasm and positive energy. I called out Vicki's name and was shocked to hear crying coming from down the hall. I hurried into the living room and spotted her sitting on a curved Dunbar Oasis sofa. She was crying her eyes out while watching *I Love Lucy* on our black and white 21-inch television.

"What's wrong, my love? I know black and white televisions are horrid, but color televisions will be available soon," I commented, trying to make her smile. Maybe she was just missing her parents. I sat down beside her and rubbed her leg in an attempt to apologize for making light of her sorrow.

"Shaun, how is this possible?" she asked the tears flowing down her cheeks.

"Baby, we went through a time portal, a wormhole if you will, with the help of the Arcturians. You will be seeing hour parents soon," I noted in the most soothing voice I could muster.

"No, Shaun, I am weeping for humanity. How did we go from this innocent society to the evil, vile world we lived in 66 years from now? I mean teenage suicides were at an all-time high, and we had an Island for the rich and famous to go to and molest young children. We had the Dark Web, where you could contract people to kill your spouse. Tearing down statues and burning buildings were a part of American life. Addiction to meth and heroin was at epic levels. Where was the sanity?" she asked, her eyes wide with emotion.

"Babe, I don't know the answer. Perhaps computers and the internet gave a voice to unhinged psychopaths and they influenced many more to come up with crazy conspiracy theories. Or maybe greed and the worshipping money robbed mankind of his soul," I said in a quiet, somber voice.

I quietly held her in my arms. Nikita Khrushchev suddenly was on the television, ranting that the Soviet Union would bury democracy and that the United States would decay from within. His words were like a prophecy. We both sat in stunned silence and realized that maybe, just maybe, Nikita Khrushchev was a time traveler too.

CHAPTER 3

V icki had to be at work early the following morning. She was extremely nervous about her shift, but I explained that the medical technology of our time was far superior to the fifties and that she would be far more advanced in her knowledge than her fellow nurses. I did warn her about standing out and drawing attention to herself because she would know things that hadn't been discovered yet.

"Just keep a low-profile, honey," I noted, reminding her of Bart's number one axiom not to bring attention to ourselves as time travelers.

"I don't care what Bart's rule says. If I can save a newborn's life with my skills, I am damn sure going to try!" Vicki replied with a fiery look in her eye. We watched *American Bandstand* and then *Father Knows Best*. We laughed at the wholesome entertainment, wondering what the folks of this generation would think of the graphically violent *Criminal Minds* or the series *Evil Lives Here* on the I.D. channel. We decided to go to the bed early and searched for our iPhones to set our alarm app when we both looked at each other and laughed.

"The only cell phones we are going find in this generation are in mental hospitals," I quipped.

We climbed into bed and held each other for a long time, trying to comfort each other, as we launched into a new reality. I was somewhat apprehensive, but my new body with its healthy heart gave me extreme confidence that our jump into the past was going to be a positive one.

The next morning, I arose early and cooked a hearty breakfast of scrambled eggs and bacon for Vicki and burned myself several times, getting acquainted with the old-fashioned kitchen appliances. I put her food on the Drexel Heritage dining room table about the same time she came downstairs.

"Ah, baby, what a surprise. I might just stay married to you when we return home." She gave me a lingering kiss, full of newlywed passion.

"Honey, you don't have to be there for an hour. Shouldn't we go back to bed and make good use of the time?" I asked.

"Ah, my Italian stallion, you are incurable. You will have to put a lid on that hot Italian passion until tonight," she said winking at me with those beautiful green eyes.

"Well, baby, you can drive our brand-new Chevy Belair then. Please remember your promise!" ashamed of my quid pro quo positioning.

When she left, I went into the living room and began to read the *Nashville Banner*, hoping to gain knowledge of the decade that I was living in and re-enforce what I already knew from my minor in history. I remember that the fifties were characterized by hard work and a drive to succeed. People wanted little government interference in their lives; however, the general population was very patriotic.

On T.V., there was some bantering between the Democrats and Republicans, but the dawn of the Cold War had defined the enemy of the Fifties as the communists, and because of that, Americans were unified and understood the simple concept united we stand and divided we fall! It was nearly 2:30 when I climbed into my room Mercury Montclair and backed out into the street. I wondered how in the hell I was going to get there by reading a map.

"Doing simple things in the 50s required more brainpower," I thought. "Perhaps that's what technology has done to us, making humans reliant on computers which diminished our thinking capabilities-- another brilliant strategy of the Annunaki."

I was on a rural state road listening to Elvis Presley's hit song "Heartbreak Hotel," wondering how my beautiful wife was doing on her very first day at the hospital when a bulletin reported that the Soviet Union was quickly building up its nuclear capacity. I knew that the Cuban Missile Crisis would not occur until 1962, and the average citizen of this generation would be petrified by that development. Some folks would soon start to build bomb shelters as the Cold War heated up. I smiled to myself, thinking that it was so ironic that the country they should be concerned about is a small, third-world country in Southeast Asia.

The landscape had changed dramatically. No busy interstates like I-40, or I-65, converging in Nashville. In fact, I remember that Dwight D. Eisenhower had passed the Federal Aid to Highways Act of 1956. Wow, my American history minor that I obtained in the future time was really paying off in more ways than I could have ever dreamed possible.

From my home in Brentwood, it would have taken me fifteen minutes to get to Union Station in my day, but today it took me almost forty-five minutes. There were barely any trucks on the road because in the fifties all commercial freight was carried by train. I gasped at the skyline of Nashville when I was crossing Victory Memorial Bridge, finished in May of 1956, on which was listed every Davidson County citizen killed in World War II.

I could smell the relative newness of the bridge, as it was just completed five months ago. I silently prayed to myself as I crossed over it. The Batman Building, Fifth Third Center Tower, and the pinnacle of the symphony building did not exist yet and since there were no Tennessee Titans, there was no football stadium. Compared to 2020, the landscape was devoid of urban sprawl. It was refreshing to see the green grass and many parks along the Cumberland River. I was looking at construction on the Life and Causality Building, Nashville's first skyscraper, as I was stopped at a traffic light when some asshole honked and then flipped me a bird because I didn't notice that the light had changed. I guess that somethings are consistent throughout time, like man's inhumanity to man and the significance of the middle finger gesture.

CHAPTER 4

I finally arrived at Union Station and found an employee parking spot. I walked across the street dodging a Ford Thunderbird as it barreled toward me blasting its horn. I caught a glimpse of a hulking blonde dude with a huge cranium and a large caveman-like forehead. He quickly hit the brakes as he pulled into the employee parking lot. I stood there, debating with myself whether to confront the bastard. I then realized it was my first day, and a fight in the parking lot would not be a good way to start off my new career.

I entered the shed which was separate from the passenger terminal. I was amazed at the volume of cargo in this 25,000 square-foot warehouse. It was comparable to the U.P.S. Shipping Centers I knew. I went to my supervisor's office.

I opened the door and was greeted by a slender man with a hawk-like nose and cold dark eyes. Ben Smith was a no-nonsense supervisor, proud of his service during the Korean War. He had pictures of his unit on his desk and on the wall. I knew that he would be a harsh taskmaster and run the place like a military installation.

"Angelo Francisco, I presume?" his eyes locked on me, and I could almost tell he was thinking I was too damn small for this demanding position. I knew that I would have to prove myself or he would let me go in a week.

Before I could say yes, he gave me a summary of the job.

'We get freight from all of the United States, for both residential and commercial customers. You will handle about 10,000 pieces of freight per shift. Think you can handle the physical demands of the job?"

"No problem," I said with a tone that was a tad bit too arrogant, perhaps covering up for my own insecurities. I had no idea what this little Italian body could do, but Shaun MacGregor never backed down from any physical task.

"We shall see. Come on. Let me introduce you to your work crew. We work in teams here, Angelo, so if you have problems working as a team, you will not work here long." He got up from the desk, and I was shocked to see that he had only one leg. I tried to avert my stare, but he noticed me glaring at his missing limb.

He strapped on an artificial leg and looked me in the eyes. With a tone of great pride, he said, "War wound. Price I paid to keep communism from spreading around the globe."

I nodded my head and thought, "Damn, the Annunaki had brainwashed every generation of man since the beginning of time. War was not fought for any idealist ideology. It was merely very profitable for the military-industrial complex controlled by the Annunaki.

We walked to my duty station, and he explained that all items received in the shed were sorted into geographical areas. My team was responsible for two specific areas.

"Your team will load the packages onto a pallet and take them to trucks that will deliver them locally. Your job is to pull the freight by pallet jack to the loading dock."

He gave instructions as we walked to meet the team. We walked to the end of the aisle and he yelled out, "Hey, Schmidt, got your pallet man!"

To my complete and utter horror, it was the same asshole that almost ran me over earlier.

Hans turned and glared at me, saying, "What the hell, Ben! We are not making pizza here. This little Italian Wop won't be able to carry the pallet one foot, much less over to the loading dock." He had a German accent.

"Give him a shot, Hans, and introduce him to the rest of the team. Right now!" Ben scowled at the big German.

Hans held up his giant hands in a universal sign of surrender and yelled, "Colin and Connor, get your potato-eating asses over here." Hans smirked, amusing himself with his reference to the Irishmen. I thought I was seeing double. Two red-headed men of forty years old appeared in front of me. They looked like they had been plucked from the streets of Dublin.

When Ben turned and left, Hans introduced us in the most unprofessional manner, "Hey, you two Micks show this Wop the ropes. Bet he don't last 30 minutes!"

I guess there is no such thing as Human Resources or nondiscrimination in the workplace back in the 1950s. Folks just did it their own way, as I remembered my old rant. There was no such thing as sexual harassment or racial discrimination, or at least no one thought about those things.

As we walked back to our work area, Connor leaned over and whispered, "Ah mate, don't let Hans get under your skin. He is just mad because he has a wee little pecker!" We laughed and bonded like brothers almost immediately. To everyone's surprise, including my own, Little Angelo pulled the heavy pallets over to the loading docks with a strength of a man twice his size because Shaun MacGregor would never let that German bastard get the best of him.

We took a lunch break at eight. Smith had a rule. All teams sit together, so I had to listen to Hans describe how he hated Blacks, who he said always wanted privileges and rights, although he did not use the term Blacks. Civil Rights was just code for spoiled coloreds like Rosa Parks and Martin Luther King, Jr., who just wanted to stir up trouble.

I kept my mouth shut, remembering what Bart had said about keeping a low profile and not drawing attention to myself, but when he mentioned how he would have taken Rosa Parks by the head of her hair and thrown her off the bus, I knew that I had to put that big Nazi in his place.

I stood up and shouted, "Listen, you big, stupid racist bastard, I got news for you. The Civil Rights movement is going to be successful, and in the future, there will be an African-American President of the United States and a lot of intelligent black women and men with advanced degrees in physics and mathematics. They would help put a man on the moon. Later," I continued, "many Blacks will serve in the Senate and Congress, and there will even be a Black woman elected Vice President of the United States."

You could have heard a pin drop. The Murphy boys looked at each other in shock, and I heard Connor say in a whisper, "Damn, that Italian bloke has gone bonkers!"

Hans just looked at me, barely containing his angry and murmuring that he would see me after work. I worked the next several hours in complete fear of that big German bastard, but I was not going to let anyone know that I was petrified. Word had spread around the warehouse that there was going to be a fight, and Connor explained that no one was betting on the fight because it was unanimous that I was going to get killed.

There was a place in the back of the shed that was like the boiler room on an aircraft carrier where men would come to settle their differences. Any actions there were ruled by a code of honor. If you showed up there, no reprisals from the company would take place. Those there were completely immune to being fired or suspended from their jobs. I walked to the back of the building, shaking like a leaf, but my male pride would not let me back down even though Hans had almost sixty pounds on me and was almost five inches taller. It was the classic David versus Goliath fight.

Hans was waiting for me when I got there. A supervisor on the second shift acted as I unofficial referee.

He said, "Gentleman, we are here to settle a workplace dispute. The two men will fight until I declare a winner. You will then stop and shake hands--if you're able."

He added the last part looking at me with a shit-eaten grin on his face. We started to circle each other, and I knew that the only strength I had was my speed. I had to stay away from his powerful mass and land quick jabs. I shocked the crowd by landing two quick right jabs to Hans's big German mug. Hans's head snapped back, and blood trickled from his nose. But my jabs only angered the beast more. His eyes bulged with hatred. I feared that I had just enraged him enough to kill me. The

Murphy brothers were wild because they hated Hans with a passion and because maybe they were spectators safe from any physical pain.

I had no idea where my boxing skill was coming from. It seemed like I had spent many hours in the gym, honing my skills. I was getting a bit cocky, and that's when my luck ended. I let Hans get too close, and he landed a thunderous right hook to my head. I felt like I had been kicked in the head by a mule. Blood spurted from my nose, and I went down like a sack of potatoes. When I came too, Hans was hovering over me ready to pounce, but the unofficial referee stopped the fight. The Murphy brothers ran to my aid and lifted me to my feet. Both men had a look of admiration in their eyes. When I begrudgingly shook Hans's hand, a look of respect flashed across his face. I was initiated that night like a member of the mob. For the next four years, my nickname was Little Rocky after Rocky Marciano, the only heavyweight fighter in history to retire undefeated.

CHAPTER 5

The Murphy brothers wanted to buy me a pint at a little Irish pub on Broadway, but I declined and told them I would take a raincheck My eyes were started to swell, and I feared they would swell shut before I could get home. When I arrived at home, it was around 12:30 a.m. I quietly opened the door and slipped into the bedroom like a phantom in the night.

Vicki was sound asleep, worn out from her first day at work, I couldn't imagine what it would be like in her department during a baby boom. I lay down next to her, careful not to wake her up and hoping that I could delay her wrath for a couple of hours at least.

Vicki turned on the bedroom light at seven a.m., excited to tell me about her first day. I struggled to open my eyes. To my horror, I could only open one eye. The left eye was completely swollen shut.

Vicki gasped in horror. "Shaun, what the hell happen to you?" I told her about the events leading to the fight behind the shed. She went to get a bag of ice to place over my eye. After she made sure that my eyes had suffered no permanent harm, she gave me a stern lecture.

"Shaun, several men gave their lives to protect you. Bart's number-one rule was for us not to mention future events and draw attention to ourselves! You violated that rule on your very first night at work. Please promise me that you will keep a low profile from this point on. Please don't let those men, our friends, die in vain, Besides, it's extremely dangerous for us." She then gave me a quick kiss on my lips and got in the shower.

I closed my one opened eye and suddenly envision John Running Bull, Bart, and Blackjack dying in the small creek. I was suddenly very ashamed of myself. I then vowed at that time never to speak of the future again. It would be a promise that I would keep for the next five years. Only then would I use the future in my mission to protect children of this generation from the demonic curse that robbed me of my soul. Unfortunately, I would be consumed by the fame and notoriety my success would bring me. Having lived the miserable, loser life of Shaun MacGregor, I would be addicted to success like a crack addict to cocaine, and success would blind me to the dangers hiding in the darkness, ready to pounce like a roaring lion.

CHAPTER 6

For the next four years, Vicki and I kept an extremely low profile. We went to work, came home, and stayed pretty much to ourselves. We marveled at the simplicity of the 1950s and enjoyed the very profitable decade when the Gross National Product would almost double. Vicki was promoted to supervisor because of her hard work and dedication to the newborn infants but also because of the special skills she learned almost seventy years in the future. I worked hard and made team leader after Hans died in a horrible car accident while he was drunk. The Murphy brothers and I drank a toast to him at their local pub. Connor held up his glass and said, "Saint Patrick, may I request that the filthy bastard burn in Hell forever!" We all clicked our glasses together and said, "Amen."

Vicki and I attended mass at the local Catholic Church with the Murphy brothers and their wives, and we all became great friends, playing the card game canasta and the board game Life by Milton Bradley. Vicki helped with the children and was immensely popular. I stayed to myself, remembering my vow to my fallen comrades.

We listened to the Million-Dollar Quartet of Elvis Presley, Johnny Cash, Jerry Lee Lewis, and Carl Perkins. We would go to movies like *The Ten Commandments*. Vicki would dress in a nice Grace Karin-like boatneck, sleeveless tea dress with a belt and matching gloves. I would be sporting a stylish hat, three-piece suit, handkerchief, coordinated tie, and wing-tip shoes. We were styling and profiling. I would whip out my Diner's Card at a classy, expensive restaurant after a movie. For me, it was a heady time to be alive.

But after four years of living in the fifties, I was getting tired of keeping a low profile. I was Italian for Christ's sake. I wanted to live large and have a zest for life. My job was mundane, and I began to yearn for the limelight. In June of 1959, the Murphy Brothers and I attended the Ingmar Johansson and Floyd Patterson fight at Yankee Stadium in New York City. It was the ultimate boy's trip as we were all big boxing fans. After all, my name was Little Rocky. Later we followed other heavyweights like Sonny Liston and, of course, the up-and-coming Cassius Clay, who later called himself Mohammed Ali. I could have made several million dollars by betting on Ingmar Johansson since the Swede was a 5-1 underdog, but that would have been ill-gotten gains, and I couldn't bring attention to myself.

At the Johansson-Patterson fight, we settled in our seats. Colin was about half drunk and his aggressive Irish temper was surging.

As soon as the fight started, he began shouting at the referee, "Come on, you dumb, blind bastard, that Swedish bloke is hitting below the belt." Connor told his brother to shut up, but the ref had had enough and ejected Colin from the stadium. It took about three security personnel to half-carry, half-drag him out.

"Should we leave, and make sure he is okay?" I asked.

"Hell, no. This trip cost me a fortune. He is a grown man, and he can take care of his own dumb arse," Connor said laughing. He himself was already three sheets in the wind, as they say. We didn't have to wait long, the bull-like Johannsson unleashed thunder and lightning, a mean left-right combination that knocked Patterson out in the third round. We were astonished by the upset and had to wash our blues away at a pub just down the street. I wished that Colin could have accompanied us there because that very night I would disclose to my drunken friend Connor that I was a fugitive time traveler, wanted by an Annunaki, an alien race that wanted me dead. That revelation was to set me on a course of destruction characterized by selfish pride and self-adoration.

We entered the pub, which was occupied by several drunk boxing fans enraged at Patterson's not being able to defend his title. Connor and I sat down at a booth in the back and began to drink our sorrows away.

"You could have beat that Swede's ass, Angelo. I can't believe Patterson got knocked out. I think that he threw the damn fight. Bookie got to him. Made him an offer he couldn't refuse," Connor said in a suspicious and paranoid tone. I didn't comment, lost in my own thoughts, wondering how much longer I would have to remain living this allusion. Connor then shocked me and opened a Pandora's box of confessions and insanity.

"I think that the Feds are after me. They are investigating me because I am from the Northern Belfast region and have affiliations with the I.R.A." Conor almost whispered the last part of his confession. I sat back astonished by his confession.

He continued, "I do not trust this government at all. After learning how they're trying to purify the gene pool by sterilizing colored women. Sounds like something Nazi Germany would do. I believe that any government that would do that is evil by controlling all humanity through surveillance. Angelo, I can't contain my thoughts about this any longer, and I am scared to death they are coming for me soon."

I studied his face for a second. It was twisted in a mask of fear, and he was trembling. That is when I decided to reveal my identity. After four years of keeping it a secret, it was a relief to finally be able to confide in another human being.

"You're just ahead of your time, Connor. America will resolve all that. But there is a lot of bad stuff coming. In 1964 President Lyndon Johnson will issue the Gulf of Tonkin Resolution, after a false attack on the *U.S.S. Maddox* and the destroyer *U.S.S. Turner Joy.* That supposed skirmish would usher in the Vietnam War, which will end up costing over 57,000 American lives. The resolution bypasses the declaration of war usually made by Congress, thus making the Vietnam War unconstitutional, an Illegal war.

Then during the war, the Central Intelligence Agency, operating as ICEX will cover up the fact that 40,000 to 80,000 servicemen fighting an illegal war thousands of miles from home, will end up addicted to heroin. The money raised by the sales of that drug will be used to fund Ngo Dinh Diem's South Vietnamese regime. In the future, Hollywood will even produce a movie called *Air American*, which will bring the covert C.I.A. operation to light. My friend, those actions will be examples of how the federal government, including the military-industrial complex, valves human life. The average American's confidence in democracy and the government will erode to a dangerous point leading to anarchy in the streets."

I kept my voice to a whisper, causing my words to be drowned out by the patrons of the noisy bar, but there was no doubt that Connor had heard me. His eyes were wide with fear and astonishment. He looked around checking to see if anyone was listening to our conversation.

When he was sure no one had heard me, he asked, "How in the hell do you know all these things. They are in the future?" he asked his eyes wide with wonder. I could tell by the expression on his face that he thought me to be insane. I calmly looked at him and told him that my name was really Shaun MacGregor and that I was a time traveler from the year twenty-first century and that I was running from an alien race that had controlled mankind from the beginning of time.

"Let's get out of here," I said. "The brief walk back to our hotel will somber us both up, and I can explain some technology to you that will blow your wee Irish mind."

I got up from the table. As we walked back to the hotel, I told him about a computer device that he could put in his pocket, the cell phone. I knew that would blow his mind because the first IBM computer would be sixteen square feet and weigh over one ton. I told him about the Internet, and how by using social media, a serial killer could lure women to their death, or a psychopath could learn how to make a bomb that people would use to blow a city block up as Eric Rudolph did in Atlanta. I told him about G.P.S., which used satellites to help drivers get from point A to point B, even if they had no idea where they were. I told him about Facebook, Twitter, Instagram, and other social media sites that would produce cyberspace relationships to give comfort to those isolated and lonely.

He gasped as I told him about operations and hormones that were used to change a man into a woman or a woman into a man and how there would be a lot of confusion about what bathroom to use. I explained how some conspiracy nuts would wear tinfoil hats because they thought the government was trying to control their minds, and how many folks thought they were being tracked by using their cell phones or chips in their credit cards. Crazies could even use the Internet to voice their displeasure with the government through unrestricted free speech, many times inciting violence and insurrection. I wanted him to know that he was on the cutting edge of the insanity to come. Finally, I told him not to utter a word to anyone about my real identity or I would tell the government about his questionable affiliations.

He just looked at me, and said, "Angelo or Shaun, or whoever the hell you are, you're either totally insane or on some powerful drugs, but your ideas are revolutionary, and you need to write a book!"

Those six simple words set me on a course that would help me create my legacy and actualize my obsession to protect innocent young lives from the demonic curse of sexual abuse.

CHAPTER 7

I was so completely obsessed with writing a book that I purchased Smith-Corona portable typewriter when I returned home from New York. I brought it to our house and set up my office in a spare room of our small suburban home. When I told Vicki that I was going to be a writer, she laughed and told me that would be awesome, like I was a child getting a new puppy. She thought that a hobby would keep me entertained and occupied so that I wouldn't be too restless in my current job.

I became obsessed with my book and thought about the plot, setting, and characters twenty-four hours a day. I would sit down and write for hours and seemed like only minutes had passed. I soon realized that I was gifted--a born writer, a prodigy. Shaun MacGregor was no longer just the Last of the Soul Searchers, but he was an artist with language, weaving a story of intrigue, action, and mystery.

I decided to write a futuristic, fictional story about 9-11 and would include some of the spy technology of that era, like malware. My main character was a no-nonsense F.B.I. agent named Jake O'Bannon, a square-jawed ex-marine. He had piercing blue eyes, a blazing temper, and a keen photographic memory. He was a quick study of others but very unorthodox and uncongenial. O'Bannon was considered a loose cannon by his superiors, but they considered him to be one of the most effective G-men ever to wear a badge. He placed many organized crime bosses behind bars for extortion, drug running, and murder because of his dogged pursuit of justice.

Early on I decided that the title of my book would be *Twin Towering Infernos of New York*. During his daily investigations, Jake would uncover evidence that would point to an ingenious conspiracy, which later would incriminate members of Congress and even the President of the United States. Jake would ask questions like why did the most powerful Air Force in the world allow a plane to crash into the Pentagon? Did our government scheme to secure oil interest in Iraq and Afghanistan and use the attack as a justification to invade those countries? Why did inside traders invest in put-options that only paid off when stock prices dropped? The stocks were American and United Airlines, and that occurred right before the disaster.

These questions made those that orchestrated 9-11 extremely nervous because Jake made no secret of what he knew, and his investigation a hit was placed on him. So, trained assassins tried to murder Jake, but because of his keen wit and fighting skills, Jake survived every attempt. At that point, Jake went rogue. He used his I.T. skills to hack into top-secret C.I.A. computer systems and get the empirical proof he needed to nail those responsible for taking over 3,000 lives that horrible September morning. Of course, I had to describe a lot of the technology I mentioned.

The manuscript ended up being over 180,000 words, and I paid over 2,000 dollars to have it edited by professionals, a fortune in the early sixties. I didn't let Vicki read the manuscript until everything was finished, fearing that she would castrate me for a gross violation of the first and most important command issued by Bart. But when she read the entire, finished novel, she was speechless, her eyes shining with pride and surprise.

"Shaun, this is brilliant, but you can't send it to a publisher! You are in gross violation of Bart's directive not to call attention to yourself as a time traveler."

"I know that I am putting our lives in danger, Vicki, but this is my calling. My gift has surfaced. I swear to you that any royalties will be kept in a foundation that offers therapeutic assistance to children who are victims of sexual abuse. I promise will not take a dime ever. Let me help the kids, Honey," I begged, looking up with hot tears streaming down my face. Being a victim of sexual abuse herself, she slowly nodded her head, and said, "God gave you this gift, Shaun, to protect his most precious creations, and I will support you with my heart, soul, and life." She then hugged me with an intensity that was unreal.

CHAPTER 8

I sent my manuscript to the ten top publishers and sat on pins and needles waiting for a response. Almost a month passed, and I almost gave up, when Doubleday, that later merged with Knopf, of the most respected book publishers in the U.S. They sent a letter of congratulations and a contract for me to sign. After that, I hired an attorney to set up a foundation called the Brocken Spectre. All royalties, including proceeds from the motion picture that would come later, would be funneled into this foundation. I, personally, would not make a dime from the book.

The novel became an immediate bestseller, selling the most copies in the year it came out. My book even outsold *The Agony and the Ecstasy* by Irving Stone. By the end of the year, it was listed as number one on *The New York Times'* Bestseller List and even earned a National Book Award.

I was flooded with interview requests but accepted only one where I revealed to my fans that all funds from the book would directly go to a foundation that was set up to help children impacted by sexual abuse. I was hoping that the knowledge that their purchase would help abused children would cause sales to explode.

I went on *Tonight Starring Jack Parr,* the number one late-night talk show on T.V. Vicki protested my appearance on the show, but my desire to help the kids outweighed Bart's rule of keeping a low profile. I was extremely nervous before the interview, but Parr's interpersonal skills put me at ease.

"Welcome, Angelo Francisco, the best-selling author of *Twin Tower Infernos of New York*," Jack told the audience as I walked across the stage. The crowd gave me an enthusiastic round of applause.

"Congratulations on your bestselling book, Angelo. I am amazed that you came out of complete obscurity to write this powerful futuristic novel. In fact, one critic called you a modern-day di Vinci for your descriptions of technology. Your account of the terrorist planes striking skyscrapers in New York was so detailed that it seemed you were there. Tell me, Angelo, are you a time traveler from the future?" he asked winking at the audience. My heart was beating so hard that I thought it would leap out of my heart, but I responded with humor.

"Yes, I am, in fact. I next will be traveling into the past and meeting with Hannibal, so I can give him some expert advice on getting those damn elephants across the Alps. So, can we speed this interview up? It takes some time and preparation to get back to 218 B.C.," I said with a goofy smile on my face. The audience exploded with laughter, and my heart slowed down a bit.

Parr roared with laughter and slapped my knee. From that point further, I was golden.

"What formalized training do you possess, a bachelor in English? Several years of writing courses? Internships with newspapers or magazines? I mean, you materialized out of nowhere, like a time traveler." Faint laughter again came from the galley. I laughed and said, "No, I went to Cornell University. There I met my beautiful wife who is a registered nurse in Nashville. After we meet, I knew that I could be a kept man, so I dropped out of school. No writing courses. I just think my writing skills are a very natural gift."

"So, like Mozart, you are a prodigy?" Parr asked shuffling his feet as if he was trying to make me brag on myself and to appear arrogant.

I just laughed it off and answered, "No, nothing like that. Besides I don't like to talk about myself." I blushed a bit and after that, the audience was like putty in my hands.

"Angelo, I understand all your royalties, all the money received from sales and future movie rights will be funneled into a foundation called

Brocken Spectre. Very unique name. Can you tell us more about this foundation?" Parr asked, his eyebrows arching.

"My foundation is set up to assist children that have been sexually abused. The program consists of what I like to refer to as enlightenment and thunder, a play on lightning and thunder. There is a treatment center in a beautiful, mountainous region. In the daytime. children will whitewater raft, hike mountain trails, climb the mountainsides, and learn orientation, first aid, and survival skills. These children will experience all the beauty that the Creator made, and he will begin to heal their trauma. At night they will go into therapy with trained psychiatrists and psychologists who specialize in helping children who have been sexually abused. They will be treated using cutting-edge, even futuristic methods. They will also have group counseling to help them realize that they are not alone." I paused for a moment, taking a deep breath. The audience was so deeply enthralled by my plans for the kids that you could hear a pin drop.

"Very impressive, Angelo. Please explain about thunder. By that term, you seem to be indicating a punishment side to your plan," Parr said in a serious, but emotional tone.

"You're on point, Jack. Sexual exploitation is a bigger issue than you think because it is decreet and covert. It is happening everywhere around you, in Boy Scouts, by the clergy and teachers. Coaches should be heavily screened. We have to "thunder" against these abusers. Although many in these fields are dedicated and would never violate a child, there is a small percentage of perverts, pedophiles, and child molesters who prey on the innocent. In the future, things will get even worse. Children will be sold like merchandise by human trafficking rings. Pedophilia will be condoned as an alternative lifestyle. I believe there will be isolated islands where the rich and famous can have sex with children. If sexual abuse goes on unchecked, we will be dealing with a raging forest fire, instead of a smoldering campfire.

"Sexual abuse needs to be nipped in the bud in this generation, and that's when the thunder comes in. I am going to hire ex-police officers, ex-F.B.I. professionals, and investigators with years of experience to hunt these demons in human camouflage down. These veterans law enforcement agents will use all their years of experience and their keen investigative strategies to uncover these bastards for what they are."

I looked right at the camera when I issued this warning. Later, when I saw a rerun of the interview, I was shocked that my sweet Italian face was a mask of rage and hatred that bordered on the psychopathic!

"Wow, that's incredible, Angelo. Tell me why you call it the Brocken Spectre Foundation?" he asked.

"First of let me explain what a Brocken Spectre is; it is a shadow of a person when the sun is behind them. The shadow has halo-like rings of colored light around it. The shadow moves as the sun hides behind the clouds or the person moves. I good friend of mine who is now deceased told me that it is the closest a human can come to seeing God here on earth," I explained, my eyes tearing up a little when I thought of Bart.

Parr looked at me for a minute. Then he asked the question that I dreaded.

"Angelo, I must ask this question. Were your sexual abused as a child? Is that where your passion for the cause originates?" Parr asked very gently.

I knew the question was coming. At first, I wanted to punch this guy in the jaw for getting so personal with me, but that was not going to help me minister to my kids.

I looked at him, smiled faintly, and spoke, "No comment."

Parr paused then held up my book and, sounding like my public relations man, said, "You can get this fantastic read at any bookstore near you." He then shook my hand and looked me in the eye and said, "It is an honor to meet you, Sir." As I walked across the floor and out of the camera's range, I could see the audience giving me a standing ovation. I then knew my ministry and legacy were no longer a dream, but they were beginning to be a reality.

CHAPTER 9

Vicki stood by me for the next six years, helping to edit the sequel to *Twin Tower Infernos of New York*. My second book entitled *The Red Scare* was another Jake O'Bannon novel. Tiring of meddling in the U.S., the Kremlin sent a cyborg to assassinate the President and Joint Chiefs of Staff. The book introduced weaponry that would make the Terminator run. Amid the heyday of the Cold War, my book would absolutely terrify its readers. Because of my extensive research, this book took me about three years to complete, and my publisher did not release it until October of 1964. The country was still in shock after the Kennedy Assassination in November of 1963, and the Vietnam Conflict was in full swing, so my publisher thought that the timing was right for my book's release.

The book, like its predecessor, was number one on the *New York Times'* Bestseller List and earned another National Book Award in February of 1965. At the same time, a movie was made of *Twin Towers Inferno*, and it was the biggest box-office revenue producer later in 1965, surpassing *The Sound of Music*. Money was pouring into the Brocken Spectre foundation, and I was invited to appear on the *James Robison Bible Show*. It was a great honor to appear with this amazing charismatic televangelist, whose preaching had led thousands of sinners to Christ.

This invitation though created great stress in my marriage to Vicki because she vehemently opposed my appearing on the show, again citing Bart.

"Shaun, it's no longer about the kids anymore. It's about your enormous ego and pride. I think that you're taking dangerous chances with our lives. That is not necessary. Your ministry in North Carolina has been operational for a year, and with your new movie and book, there is more than enough money pouring into the foundation."

"That's true, Vicki, but think of how much money that it will take to hire trained therapists and retired investigators for the center. It is essential that I raise as much money as possible because we don't know when the Arcturians will be coming for us," I said in a pouting and elevated tone.

As Vicki stormed out of the room, she yelled, "If you keep taking these reckless risks, it will be the Annunaki that will come for you!"

As I now reflect on her prophecy, I realize that she was correct. After living the life of the loser Shaun MacGregor for years, I was intoxicated by the fame and fortune that characterized Angelo Francisco's life. Vicki's prediction would come true in less than 48 hours, and I would be thrust into the third dimension of hell. It would take my sanity, threaten my life, and force me into a vile, horrifying existence.

Chapter 10

Aweek before going on James Robison's show, a freak accident occurred in which Connor Murphy was killed. He was chocking the wheels of the trailer after a driver backed it against the dock. Chocking the tires acts as an emergency brake of sorts while the trailer is being loaded. Through some supernatural energy, the chock slipped, and the trailer rolled forward, trapping Connor underneath. Connor was crushed. His heart was squeezed and burst like an overgrown pimple. I discovered the body and was horrified by the thought that the mysterious death was due to his knowing my identity. The safety folks investigated the incidental and ruled that Connor Murphy's death was accidental. But I still felt so much guilt that I almost canceled my appearance on Robison's show, but my taste for national exposure and fame overrode my grief.

The show was live and again a felt that twinge of nervousness as I worked across the stage. He announced me as the saint that had opened a treatment center for sexually abused children in the North Carolina mountains, adding to my nervous trepidation because I knew that Shaun MacGregor was no saint. My heart began to calm when I realized the audience would see a charming little Italian man with a huge heart, instead of the drunken wreck of a human being.

The audience gave me a standing ovation again.

"Thank you for coming, Angelo. Since its inception, your treatment center has treated over 10,000 of God's most precious creations--his children. Could you tell the audience where your treatment center is, and how they can send a loved one there if they find themselves in such need. I understand there is no cost to the families whatsoever."

"That's right. The treatment center is free to any child, regardless of economic status. But, unfortunately, right now there no room at the inn. We are completely booked for the next two years, but we are taking requests for 1966. The treatment center is approximately thirty miles from Ashville, North Carolina, and is on the shores of a beautiful mountain lake. The residential hall and counseling center are on a sloping mountain bluff overlooking the lake. A large cross stands above the lake and is illuminated at night. This special place is of spiritual significance to many clients. It is an outdoor sanctuary that makes them feel closer to their Creator. There are walking trails around the lake and a footbridge that crosses over the lake. Kayaking, canoeing, and fishing are available whenever the children are not in counseling sessions. During the day, children can also be involved in whitewater rafting down the French Broad River, hiking to waterfalls on the Horsepasture River, or climbing the winding natural staircase at Chimney Rock," I said taking a breath, trying to dial back my excitement.

"Angelo, I understand that your treatment center has prevented many suicides and comforted many destressed children. Because of you, instead of hiding their sexual trauma and masking their pain with drugs and alcohol, many face their demons, conquer them, and turn to God. Praise God. Hallelujah!" Robison then shouted! I then explained to James, that God given gifts, like my writing ability should be used to bring glory to God. Too many people use their gifts to acquire worldly possessions, and power.

"Angelo, I am concerned about the thunder part of your Brocken Spectre Foundation, in which you go after the abusers. in Romans 12:19, the Lord makes it clear that vengeance is his responsibility. Don't you think that hunting down pedophiles is vigilante justice?" Robison asked, putting his hand on his King James Bible. Anglo speaking-James, I believe that God given gifts, like my writing ability should be used to glorify God. Too many people use their gifts for greed, power of selfish pursuit of Worldly possessions.

"Mark, there are plenty of examples of our God using people to fulfill his vengeance, like David slaying a giant, professional-trained soldier such Goliath. This is only an example of that principle. We prefer to be tools, mighty hammers for God!" I shouted with passion.

"One final question, Angelo. Have you have been abused? Is that why you're so passionate about helping kids?" the preacher asked, his voice laced with compassion and empathy.

I looked at him for a long time and then answered,

"I believed that God allows Satan to wound your soul, and although this wound causes God great pain, He allows these bad things to occur because he knows that's where your motivation for your ministry lies. Why do you think alcoholics are sponsors for other folks lost in the clutches of alcoholism? Or why parents that have children that go missing help one another? I will let that thought answer your question," I said, wanting this interview to be over.

Robison paused and let me gather my emotions.

"Let us pray for this Godly man and his foundation," he then said, bowing his head reverently. I listened to his prayer.

Then out of nowhere, my alien father's voice drowned out Robison's voice with seven words that formed an unholy prophecy, "Tonight we are coming for you, Shaun!"

CHAPTER 11

When I returned to Nashville and pulled up in the driveway, Vicki was standing at the door. She opened the door and ran to hug me.

"Honey, I am so proud of you. Your interview was intense, and viewers could almost feel your passion and commitment to the kids. Please let this be your last interview though because I'm very scared." she whispered in my ear. I looked into her eyes and suddenly was very ashamed of myself for putting her through all this. She had been my rock for the past ten years.

"I promise, my love. That will be my last interview because the foundation will have enough revenue from the books, movies, and from private donations from others who are sympathetic to the cause. Now, what's for dinner, Hon?" I asked stroking her beautiful dark red hair.

"Well, my dear, I'm cooking some lasagna, my Italian stallion." She laughed then added, "Please don't eat too much. Plans for you later tonight."

I picked her up and carried her across the threshold like a new husband with his most precious soulmate for life. After dinner, we made passionate love. Afterwards, exhausted, we drifted off to sleep.

CHAPTER 12

I woke to my nightstand vibrating and bright lights sweeping down from the ceiling. Then I heard Bart's deep bass voice

"Old Hoss, you violated my number one rule too many times. Now we are here to take you back to the Annunaki, and you will pay for your insubordination with your flesh and blood!"

I managed to open my eyes, an action I will regret for all eternity, Bart's face was inches from mine, his saliva dripping off his chin and pooling on my neck. I screamed, and he started laughing and stood up beside my bed. His face was hideous, a half-human and half-grizzly bear. His teeth were chiseled into fangs, and there was a bright letter A engraved on his forehead. His eyes were blood red and seemed to glow in the darkness.

Standing beside him was Connor Murphy, eyes glowing, his head spinning on his shoulders like a deranged gyro. He was chanting, "It's your fault the Annunaki found me, Shaun. They changed me, Shaun, and now you're going to pay with your soul." He stared at me with blood squirting from his eyes, drenching my face and soaking the pillow I was lying on.

I looked past these things, what must have been Annunaki cyborgs, and my fear intensified because Hans was crawling on the ceiling and was trying to use a laser to cut a hole in it. He looked at me with black eyes, darker than the deepest pits of hell.

"Hey, you little Wop," he said. "Long time, no see. Got to finish my job here cutting a hole in the ceiling so that the Annunaki tractor beam can carry you away like a piece of shit," he laughed, and his two fellow Annunaki henchmen joined in, sounding like some choir at the gates of hell.

As the beam started to lift me into the air, I screamed and kicked my legs as Chris Dermott had done in his intervention. As I looked down at Vicki, I thought that I would see a look of sheer terror and concern for me on her face, but instead below the carved A on her forehead were glowing eyes and a faint smile on her sensuous lips.

PART 4
Epilogue or Back Home Again

Present Day

CHAPTER 1

I woke up, my hair soaking wet, and my body drenched in sweat. When consciousness invaded my brain, I realized that my vision had been a horrific nightmare. I breathed a sigh of relief and reached over to cuddle Vicki, but she was not there.

"Probably cooking breakfast," I thought. I need to scratch my nose, but when I tried to lift my left hand, it would not budge. I panicked and looked over at my hand expected to see a bloody stump, but to my amazement, I was handcuffed to the bed.

I yelled and kicked in a fit of rage. I managed to look in the mirror at that point and was shocked to see the face of Shaun MacGregor staring back at me. A burly male nurse came into my room and roughly grabbed my arm. He then stuck me with a needle and injected a medication that calmed me immediately. Before I drifted off the sleep, I asked, Where the hell am I?"

He simply looked at me and said matter of factly, "You're at Western Kentucky State Mental Hospital in Hopkinsville, Kentucky."

"Get me out of here. I haven't done a damn thing," I shouted at the top of my lungs.

"Well, my man, all the evidence seems to suggest that you are a psychopathic serial killer wanted for killing at least five men." He then looked at me like I had an eye in the middle of my forehead. I was about to grab him with my good arm and kill a sixth man when I surrendered to the darkness as it encased my brain.

I was in and out of consciousness for I don't know how long, but during a lucid period, I heard the doctor talking with an F.B.I. agent. I decided to play 'possum so I could gather some information.

"When can I question him about the murders?" the FBI agent asked, his voice sounding a lot like Bart's. I wanted to open my eyes but was in fear that they would notice by alertness.

"Your suspect is extremely sick; I think he is either suffering from schizophrenia or dissociative personality disorder. One minute he claims to be Angelo Francisco from the 1960s, and the next minute he is Shaun MacGregor, the last soul searcher on Earth, whatever the hell that means. That's nothing new around here though, Captain America and Spiderman currently reside here as well."

The doctor giggled as his own humor. Perhaps he had been here a little bit too long himself, I thought.

Dr. Obrien cleared his throat and continued. "Shaun has had a very troubled past. He suffered sexual trauma at an early age and a lifetime of perceived rejection from his stepfather. He is antisocial, and he hates authority because authority reminds him of his controlling stepfather. All his victims are male. In his mind he is killing his stepfather again and again," Dr. Obrien continued, peering intently at the G-man.

Bart then spoke, "All three men had been charged with sexual abuse of children but had been found not guilty by the courts. Seems like ole Shaun was serving up some type of vigilante justice of his own. What is scary is that Shaun researched and stalked these men with great intensity, totally consumed by a hatred formed in the bowels of hell. Thanks, old hoss," Bart reverted to his favorite nickname. "Call me as soon he is half-way sane."

He then paused but continued, "We had been tracking this creep for a couple of days after he murdered his uncle. During our investigation, we discover that he may have been a driver for hire with the nasty habit of killing his clients. On October 27th, he jumped off Seventy Six Falls to evade us. We found him on the verge of hypothermia in an abandoned lake house on Lake Cumberland three whole days after he jumped from the 80-foot waterfall. Must have tried to drown himself several times. At that time, he claimed to be a famous writer from the 1960s. We normally take them right to jail, but this unsub is so deranged we pulled some strings to have him sent here, hoping that you could get him sane enough to confess to the murders so we could have him tried and convicted."

"Well, I have him on a Risperidone-Lamotrigine drip. When he is sane enough for an interview, I will call you immediately. He should have some clarity in a couple of days . . . if he ever does."

"Thanks, Hoss," the G-man said. When I heard that expression again, I just had to peek. I opened my eyes, and sure enough, the doppelganger of Bart stood near the door. I then realized that all this was a vast conspiracy directed by the Annunaki to make me appear to be insane and thus end my threat to them.

CHAPTER 2

I woke up to the Bart clone standing over my bed, and my sixth sense warned me that something had changed. Standing beside him was a man that was the spitting image of Colin Murphy. I felt like Dorothy in *The Wizard of Oz* when she woke up from her trip down the Golden Brick Road.

"My name is Brocken Spectre, and this is Johnny O'Toole, my partner. We are here to question you about the murders of Chris Dermott, Ben Dixon, and Ron Mears. Their bodies were found off I-65 by some deer hunters. The bodies were near each other, buried in shallow graves, each killed with a double-tap with one round to the head and one to the chest execution-style. All three of the bodies had your D.N.A. on them. The murder weapon was a 9mm, a gun registered to you, Shaun. Can you explain that?" He asked thinking that I was on the verge of confessing.

I lay there trying to suppress my rage, trying not to act insane, but then I thought, "What the hell. It's a lot easier to break out of a mental hospital than a prison."

"Listen to me, Bart. I know you're back under the control of the Annunaki. You are a freaking cyborg, so I am not telling you shit. I am being framed by your puppet master, my alien stepfather," I said in my most aggressive voice.

The Colin clone looked at his boss and said, "This dude is bat-shit crazy. Let's not waste time on him. He going to get an automatic pass to the nuthouse. No shrink is going to find him sane enough to stand trial."

"That's right, you Colin look-alike bastard. Oh, you probably don't recognize me. I'm Angelo Francisco, your best friend from the 1960s. Famous author. My books *Red Scare*, and *Twin Tower Infernos of New York* were on the New York bestseller list for a year." He just looked at me with a slight smirk, as if he were enjoyed being entertained by a certifiable crazy person.

"Shaun, the bodies we found were fairly decomposed, meaning the men were killed before you beat your uncle to death after he confronted you about dating your best friend's girl. Seems that he had a code of honor that you violated. All the victims but him had one thing in common, Shaun. Do you know what that is?" the persistent Bart clone asked.

"No, but I'm sure your traitor ass is going tell me," I said staring defiantly at his increasingly agitated mug.

"You were their Goober driver, taking them on their last rides. Somehow you knew these men lived by themselves and that they were professionals who spent many hours traveling across the country alone. You knew no one would report them missing for days."

"Listen to me, dumb ass. I am the last soul searcher on Earth. I turned those vicious bastards into harmless clones. Instead. Of committing hideous crimes, they will benefit humanity. I should be getting a frigging medal. I am in the middle of an alien battle between the Arcturians and Annunaki for the domination of Earth." My voice started to increase in volume, veins popping out of my forehead.

The Bart cyborg FBI agent shook his head, "Shaun, we found two bodies burnt nearly beyond recognition above Seventy Six Falls, one was a native American Indian and one a black man. They were just fishing on Indian Creek, minding their own business, and someone killed them. The coroner puts the time of death some time on Thursday afternoon, October 27th, the same time you jumped from the falls. Shaun, I am not buying your performance today, and I am personally making sure you are put down like the rabid dog you are."

Bart turned to leave.

The Colin clone turned and gleefully said, "Shaun, I Googled your book titles and you're correct. They were bestsellers and were extraordinarily successful. In fact, both were made into movies, but they were not written by any Angelo Francisco, but rather by a dude name Hans Schmidt. He was a great dude too. Donated all his money to a foundation that helped kids that have been sexually abused."

I don't really remember what happened next. The disappointment and fury erupted simultaneously. My legacy had been stolen from me. The rage was blinding. I screamed and was kicking like a maniac. The Bart and Colin clones hurried out of the room. Four or five orderlies came and held me down as the burly nurse grabbed my arm and dangerously inserted a needle full of Librium into my brachial artery, thus sending me into much-welcomed oblivion.

I woke up nearly twelve hours later to my Aunt Jackie stroking my hand. Pee Wee was standing behind her, and both were forgiving me for my evil transgressions.

"Shaun, I forgive you for what you did to your Uncle Jim. I know you loved him. You are just mentally ill, and I will be on your side until this crisis is over," Aunt Jackie said rubbing my hand. I jerked my hand away and yelled at her

"Stay away from me, you Annunaki clone. You just want to spy on me, so you can report back to my alien stepfather." Somehow, I freed my hand from the handcuffs, put them around her neck, and started choking her. The Pee Wee clone tried to help her, but I kicked him in the groin, and he fell on the floor gasping for breath. I let go of her and jumped to my feet just as two orderlies came rushing in to subdue me. I hit one with a bedpan and swung a round, left uppercut into the jaw of the other, all the time yelling at them to check along Aunt Jackie's scalp for the incision that would prove her brain was missing and that she was an Annunaki clone. I was able to get out the door, and that's when the police officer that was posted at the door tased me and used his billy club to knock my lights out.

I woke up in a padded cell with a straight jacket on. My head was throbbing, and my eyes were swollen shut. I sat there stunned, trying to make sense of the last twenty-four hours. One minute I'm a famous writer voted *Time*'s man of the year for my philanthropist spirit, and the next I'm lying in a mental hospital. For the first time, I wondered where Vicki and Judge were, and my heart began to yearn for them. I thought maybe they were still trapped back in the 1960s and was almost glad because they wouldn't see me in this sad, sick condition.

I began to weep. My heart was breaking. I was sobbing when suddenly a ray of right pierced my small cell and the voice of John Running Bull spoke to my heart. "Get up, Shaun, my son. You are the only hope for humanity. Millions will perish if give up now. Remember what the Bible says in Luke 12:48, 'For everyone who has been given much, much more will be asked.' Honor me and the others that gave our lives for your survival."

I could imagine all that would go on after that. I stood up and raised my clenched fist to the heavens and said, "I, Shaun MacGregor, The Last Soul Searcher, will escape with the help of the Arcturians. I will seek revenge on my stepfather! So help me God!"

CHAPTER 3

A week later, while under the sedation of my new friends--Olanzapine and Lamotrigine--I went on a little trip and never left the sanitarium. I had an out-of-body experience like some experience in near-death episodes.

As I floated high above the trees, I was just amazed by how vivid the vision appeared. The winding road to my stepfather's home was lined with sugar maples that were ablaze with orange, crimson, and salmon pink. The babbling brook that meandering along the wood line was an amazing, brilliant YinMn Blue. I then thought of the vision that the Apostle John had as he wrote the book of Revelation on the Island of Patmos. How terrifying those visions of twentieth-century weapons must have been to people of the day.

It was a bright November morning. I saw Mad Dog MacGregor sitting on the dock by his retention pond. He was relaxing, his mission almost complete. His hair was blowing in the cool wind, and the warm sunshine was caressing his skin. Mad Dog sat in complete silence, staring at the brilliant sunlight as it danced on the still waters. He appeared to be deep in thought or meditating.

The large figure of a man who moved like a programmed machine appeared behind him. For a moment I hoped it was an Arcturian assassin seeking revenge. The shadow that the giant figure cast did not alarm Mad Dog because he knew it was his favorite killing machine.

My auditory senses were just as keen as my vision, and I heard the machine-man say, "Sir, it was genius to order the clones of his Aunt

Jackie and best friend to visit the Arcturian slave in the hospital. He went wild and attacked two orderlies before the officer that I posted at the door knocked him out cold. He presently resides in a padded cell and is fitted with a straight jacket." Bart's voice was flat, drone-like.

"Very good, Bart, I want you to monitor my stepson's progress and make sure that certain episodes of uncontrollable anger and rage occur periodically, which may mean adjusting the medications occasionally. I want him kept there until the completion of our plans to convert the Earth to our new home. It's good to have you back, Bart. Sorry I had to liquidate your assets. Just a debt collector protecting my investment!" He then nodded his head, arrogantly dismissing his drone, his machine clone, and the ultimate puppet.

The supreme leader relaxed and was contemplating his phenomenally successful mission when he heard lighter footsteps. Nearby a very female voice called out, "Father?"

He knew that his daughter--his love and protégée--was directly behind him. My heart was beating hard as I watched. My soul was fractured by the ultimate betrayal. The love of my life was the daughter of the most hideous creature in the galaxy! I cringed as I saw my dog Judge standing obediently by her side.

Are there no bounds to this treason?" I thought.

I listened to their sordid conversation as I realized that, I Shaun MacGregor was truly sleeping with the enemy!

"Hello, Vicki, or Cassandra, or whatever the earthlings are calling you today!" Mad Dog MacGregor laughed. She stood beside him with that very handsome-looking Springer spaniel beside her.

"Father, was that Bart I saw leave here?"

"Yes, dear, he was reporting on the Arcturian slave. Why?"

"Are you sure we can trust him?" Vicki asked.

"Sure, he is fine. Doesn't remember a thing. We just reprogramed him. He is the same killing machine that we initially created. Don't you worry your pretty little head."

Mad Dog then noticed the four-legged creature standing by his daughter as if he were guarding her.

"Where did you get that fine animal?" Mad Dog asked.

"Oh, just a reminder of the miserable Arcturian slave that you forced me to endure for the last ten years. Why did it take so long to find us, father? I wore that tracking device every hour of every day," Vicki said with her mouth wrinkled up like she had eaten something very sour.

"Well, dear, there are many wormholes in space filled with many dimensions and time warps. We worked as fast as possible, but you were really only missing for three days," Mad Dog answered in an annoyed voice.

"My dear daughter, you are a super spy, born with the gift from your father. You can cloak yourself to such a great degree that humans accept you and trust you completely. I could have never pulled this off without you! By telling me about that listening device in the library, I was able to trick Bart into doing the time jump at Seventy Six Falls where the Arcturians' craft would have little protection. I used Shaun to lead us to that damn Indian Arcturian sympathizer, finally getting rid of that royal pain in my ass. Honey, do you remember that thunderous roar you heard as you were falling off the waterfalls?"

"Yes, vaguely, Father," Vicki replied.

"Well, honey, that was all part of the mission. We ambushed that Arcturian warcraft, killing over 5,000 of our enemy. It was an incredibly successful day for all Annunaki. We finally got even with those snowflakes for meddling in our affairs. The coverup could not have been done without you either, honey. We used the gun that you stole from Shaun to kill those three Earth clones. Then we planted the D.N.A., fibers, and hair that you provided us. I am enormously proud of you, my daughter!" Mad Dog Mike said as the sun illuminated the pride in his eyes.

"My daughter, I had my eyes on you since your birth. I knew your teenage years were troubled, and when you got in a bad spot selling drugs as a young adult, I knew I had to intervene. When that Earthling judge ordered you to enter the military or go to jail, I pulled some strings to get you into my command in San Antonio, Texas," Mad Dog said as if he was in a trance, remembering those days so many years ago.

"Yes, father, I thought you to be a weird, crazy man then when you told me of abducting my mother and impregnating her with your seed.

I was going to report you to the military police for harassment--until you told me of the birthmark on my mother's hip and the tattoo on her lower back that I affectionately referred to as her tramp stamp," Vicky said laughing.

"Father, you're a wicked genius! You created me for this very mission, didn't you?" Vicki asked, amusement in her eyes.

"Yes, my dear, I will not lie to you. We created you to counteract the damage that was being done by the Arthurian slave. He is technically your half-brother since he was my stepson, but don't worry. Incest is not recognized on our planet!" Mad Mike laughed so hard that he almost inhaled oxygen, which would have instantaneously killed him.

Mike then grabbed his daughter's hand and brought her close to him as he whispered in her ear that it was time for some father and daughter bonding time. Vicki laughed.

They both watched the setting sun as it slipped beyond the horizon. I thought an innocent onlooker would have interpreted the scene as a tender moment between father and daughter or between two lovers, but really, they were two vile, treacherous aliens planning the demise of all humanity.

The pain welled up in my heart as the vision ended, but at that moment, I swore to the deceased souls of my dear Aunt Jackie, Uncle Jim, and best friend Pee Wee that I would escape this hell hole and seek unholy vengeance against all those that sought to destroy mankind.

The End